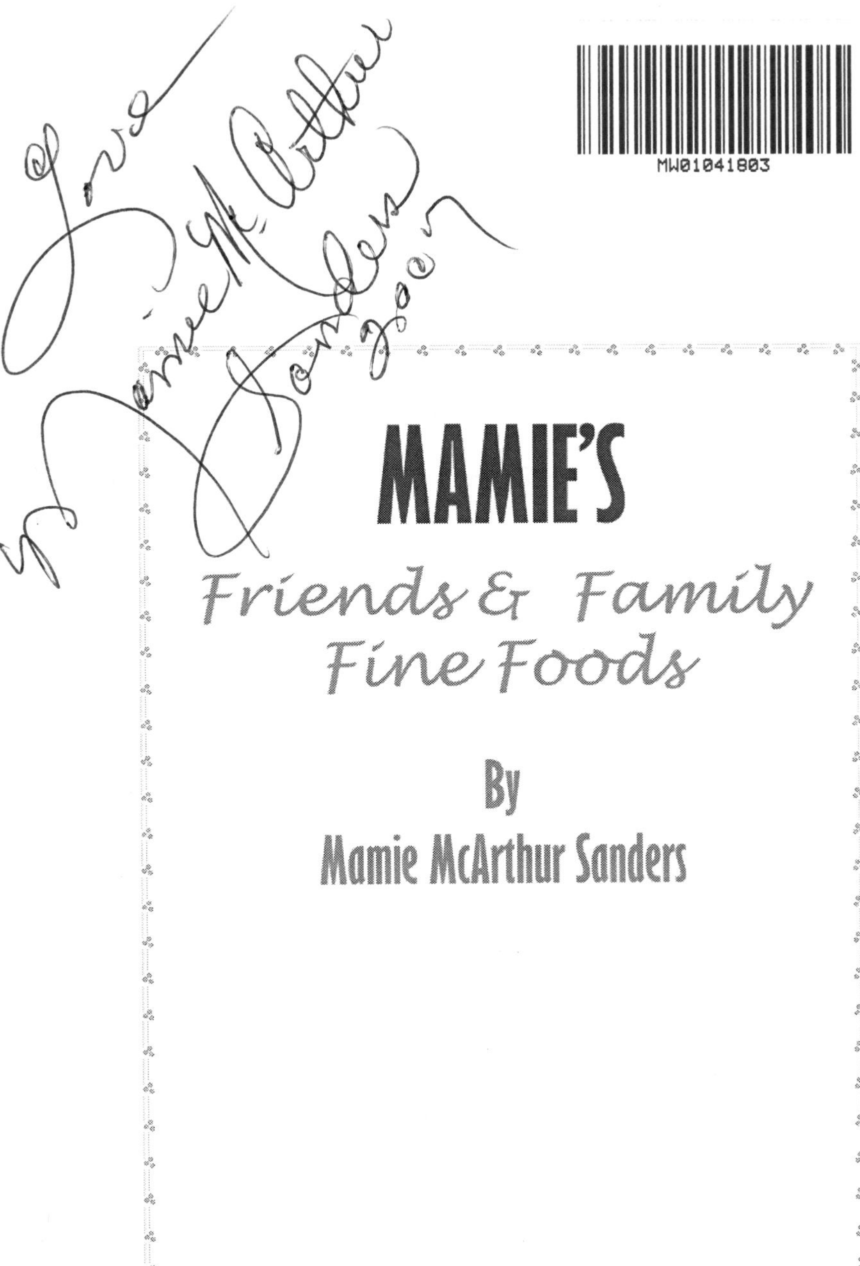

MAMIE'S

Friends & Family Fine Foods

By

Mamie McArthur Sanders

Westview Publishing Co., Inc. - Nashville, Tennessee

© by Mamie McArthur Sanders

All Rights Reserved. No portion of this book may be reproduced in any fashion, whether electronic or mechanical, without the express written consent of the author.

Printed in the United States of America on acid-free paper.

ISBN 1-933912-00-6

Layout and recipe organization by Nelda Bates.

Pre-press by Westview Publishing Co., Inc.

Westview Publishing Co., Inc.
8120 Sawyer Brown Rd., Ste. 107
Nashville, Tennessee 37221
www.westviewpublishing.com

CONTENTS

Every little girl wants to grow up to be "just like her Mother". I thank God for mine, and it is with pride and love that I dedicate this cookbook to her - my friend and Mom - Christine Wilson.

MAMIE'S MEMO

AT LAST, WE HAVE A COOKBOOK!

When we started this project last Spring by sending you a recipe for the "Happiness Cake," I don't think we had any idea that we would receive such an outpouring of support and enthusiasm.

Two Hundred and twenty of you wonderful people have shared with us two hundred and seventy-three of your favorite recipes. Three were submitted without a name and we have designated these as "Mystery Chefs."

We are proud to publish these recipes as a part of "Mamie's Friends and Family Fine Food" and we thank you so very much. It has been our pleasure.

Brent and I have, indeed, been blessed throughout the years just by knowing and working with you – our friends and family. We sincerely hope you will enjoy this cookbook. It is YOURS!

With much love,

"MAMIE"

Mamie

Acknowledgements

My gratitude goes to my editor and good friend of more than thirty years, Nelda Bates, and to the rest of my great staff here at McArthur Sanders – Debbie Clark, Sherri Costes, Melissa Davis, Genice Johnson, and Sue Pratt. Ladies, I know how active each of you were in getting this project "off the ground" and being there when your help was needed. You are my rock – and I want you to know how much I appreciate and need you!

My appreciation and a special "thank you" to Jean Caillouette for pitching in at the "last minute" to help her friend, the editor, with all the final details.

My heart-felt love to my husband, Brent, and the rest of my family for their constant support and encouragement.

7065 Moores Lane
Brentwood, TN 37027
615-370-4663
www.mcarthursanders.com

APPETIZERS/DIPS

Notes...

ARTICHOKE BREAD APPETIZER

1 loaf frozen bread dough
1 pkg. Genoa salami or pepperoni
1 pkg. sliced Swiss cheese
1 jar marinated artichoke hearts
sweet mustard
garlic salt/garlic powder
dried oregano/basil
Parmesan cheese

Let bread dough rise at room temperature according to package instructions. Lightly spray a cookie sheet with cooking spray. Roll thawed bread dough out onto a cookie sheet into a rectangular shape. Spread oil from the marinated artichoke hearts on bread dough. Sprinkle a little garlic salt/powder and herbs over half of the bread dough.

Layer Swiss cheese on dough. Top with salami or pepperoni and spread a little mustard over salami. Top with Swiss cheese.

Cut artichoke hearts in half. Place on top of cheese. Spread a little more oil over all. Sprinkle a little more garlic salt/powder and herbs. Sprinkle with Parmesan cheese.

Fold long ends of dough over to center and pinch to close. Spread artichoke oil over top of loaf. Sprinkle with herbs and Parmesan.

Bake at 350 degrees for 15 minutes. Cut on the diagonal and serve. This is also excellent with a salad.

Judy Smith

ARTICHOKE DIP

8 oz. cream cheese
1 can artichoke quarters
Parmesan cheese (grated)
1 stick butter or margarine
Triskets

1. Drain artichoke quarters and place in bottom of pie plate, chopping them up a bit more.
2. Microwave cream cheese and butter together until butter is melted. Mix the butter and cream cheese together until very smooth, spread on top of the artichokes.
3. Sprinkle parmesan cheese generously on top.
4. Bake at 350 degrees for 20-30 minutes or until hot and bubbly. (This can also be heated in a microwave.)
5. Spread on Triskets.

Pat Iannacone

BRIE CRISPS

4 oz. brie cheese without rind
1/8 tsp. salt
2 dashes cayenne
2/3 c. flour
½ c. butter at room temp.

Combine cheese and butter in food processor. Add other ingredients and process until dough almost forms a ball. Shape into a roll 2 inches round and wrap in plastic. Refrigerate or freeze overnight. Slice very cold rolls into ¼ inch thick slices. Place 2 inches apart on cookie sheet and bake at 400 degrees for 10-12 minutes until edges are slightly browned. Cool on a rack. Sprinkle lightly with paprika and serve.

Great "keep in freezer" item for instant entertaining.

.

Cathy Marston.

CALIFORNIA CAVIAR

When I relocated to Tennessee, I learned that it is a tradition to eat blackeyed peas on New Year's Day. There is only one recipe that I ever made that used blackeyed peas. It is health-conscious and delicious. Enjoy!

1 small jar Pace picante sauce (mild or medium)
2 cans blackeyed peas, drained (16 oz.)
1 can shoepeg corn, drained (16 oz.)
1 c. diced green bell pepper
2 c. chopped fresh tomato
2 tsp. freshly ground pepper
1 c. chopped white onion
¼ c. chopped fresh cilantro
½ can diced black olives

Mix all the ingredients together well and marinate in the refrigerator for 24 hours. Serve with tortilla chips, baked pita or toasted baguettes. Enjoy!

Lisa Smith

CAROL'S APPETIZER

4 cans blackeyed peas, (washed and drained)
1 green pepper, diced
1 tsp. chopped garlic in jar
1 tsp. sugar
1 bottle Italian Dressing
I large jar pimento (drained)
1 onion, diced
jalapeno peppers (in jar) chopped as you desire

Marinate at least 24 hours. Only gets better as it sits. Leave in refrigerator. Serve with "Frito Scoops".

Carol Schmidt

CHEESE BALL

2 (8 oz.) pkg. cream cheese - softened
1 tbsp. grated onion
1 jar Old English spread
1 tbsp. lemon juice
chopped pecans

Beat cream cheese well. Add Old English Spread and mix well with onion and lemon juice. Chill.

Form into ball. Coat with pecans. Chill additional 2-4 hours (or longer). Serve with assorted crackers.

Lynn Babcock

CRABBIES

1 jar Kraft Old English Cheese Spread
1 stick butter, softened
1 ½ tsp. mayonnaise
½ tsp. garlic salt
½ tsp. seasoned salt
1 can crab meat (7 oz.)
1 pkg. halved English muffins

MIX: cheese, butter and mayo with electric beater. Add rest of ingredients.

SPREAD: on muffins and cut into quarters.

FREEZE: at least 10 minutes on cookie sheet.

Ready to eat or freeze in baggies. Cook on broil 8" from heat until bubbly (5-8 minutes).

Claudia Berry

HAM & CHEESE APPETIZERS

6 oz. cream cheese, softened
1 egg
2 tbsp. milk
1 pkg. crescent rolls
1 c. ham (small pieces)
½ c. medium cheddar cheese (shredded)
½ pkg. Hidden Valley ranch mix

Blend cream cheese, cheddar cheese, egg and milk. Add seasoning ham and ranch mix. Place crescent rolls in muffin pans. Add 1 tbsp. filling per muffin. Makes 36. Bake at 350 degrees for 15 minutes.

Judy Stanford

HOLIDAY CHEESE BALL

2 – 8 oz. pkg. cream cheese
2 tbsp. green pepper
½ c. crushed pineapple (drained)
2 tsp. salt
2 tbsp. onion
2 cups pecans (crushed)

Mix all ingredients together except 1 cup of pecans.
Form into a ball, and then roll ball in the remaining cup of pecans.
.

Pam Greer

HOT ARTICHOKE SPREAD OR DIP

1 can artichoke hearts (14 oz.) drained & chopped
1 c. grated parmesan cheese
1 c. real mayonnaise
½ tsp. garlic powder

Combine all ingredients, mix well. Spoon into a lightly greased casserole dish, Bake at 350 degrees for 25 minutes. Serve with Scoops by Frito Lay. This family favorite won't last long!

Mary Jo Bates

HOT BEEF DIP

¼ c. chopped onion
1 c. milk
2 (3 oz.) pkgs. smoked sliced beef, chopped
2 tbsp. dried, chopped parsley
¼ c. Parmesan cheese
1 tbsp. butter
8 oz. pkg. cream cheese
4 oz. can chopped mushrooms, drained
Garlic salt to taste

Saute chopped onions in 1 tablespoon butter. Add milk, cream cheese, chopped beef, mushrooms, Parmesan cheese, parsley and garlic salt. Stir and boil over medium heat. Great served with French bread or Ritz crackers.

DeLacy Bellenfant-Layhew

HOT SPINACH DIP

2 (10 oz.) pkg. frozen chopped spinach.
1/2 c. chopped onion
1 pickled jalapeno, chopped (optional)
2 c. shredded Monterey Jack cheese
1/3 c. half and half
1 tsp. hot sauce
8 oz. cream cheese, softened
1 (11 oz.) can chopped tomatoes with green chiles
1 c. chopped fresh tomatoes
salt to taste

Preheat oven to 350 degrees. Thaw spinach and press to remove excess moisture. Combine the spinach with the onion, jalapeno, cream cheese, shredded cheese, half and half, hot sauce and canned tomatoes with green chiles in a bowl; mix well. Fold in fresh tomatoes. Spoon into greased 2 quart baking dish. Bake for 20-30 minutes or until bubbly. Serve with baked tortilla chips or crackers.

Jan Crowe

HOT SPINACH AND ARTICHOKE DIP

2 -14 oz. cans artichoke hearts, drained and chopped
½ c. frozen spinach, thawed and drained
¾ c. mayonnaise
¾ c. Parmesan cheese
salt and pepper to taste
Tostado chips or crackers

Preheat oven to 350 degrees. In a large bowl, mix together the artichoke hearts, mayonnaise and Parmesan cheese. Add spinach and salt & pepper to taste.

Pour mixture into decorative corning dish that can be used to bake in and then used to serve. Bake for 25 minutes or until top is golden brown. Serve with chips (Tostado) or crackers. Serves 4-6.

Madonna Mitchell

LAYERED NACHO DIP

Combine 1 can (16 oz.) refried beans and ½ package Taco seasoning mix and spread in 11x7 inch dish. Layer with the following ingredients in order listed:

1 carton avocado dip (6 oz.) or 1 c. guacamole dip
1 carton sour cream (8 oz.).
1 can chopped ripe olives, drained (4 ¼ oz.)
2 tomatoes, diced
1 finely chopped small onion
1 can chopped green chilies, not drained (4 ½ oz.)
6 oz. shredded Monterey Jack or Cheddar Jack cheese

Serve with corn chips. Yield: 8 cups

Sara Jo White

PHILLIPPA'S CHEESE WAFERS

1 ½ lbs. shredded cheddar cheese
1/3 tsp. cayenne pepper
1/3 tsp. salt
3 sticks butter
2 ½ c. flour

Preheat oven to 350 degrees. Mix dry ingredients with shredded cheese. Melt butter and add to mixture, blending thoroughly. Using a melon scoop, form mixture into balls. Place on ungreased cookie sheet and flatten into circle.

Bake 30 minutes or until crisp.

Trudy Byrd

PIMENTO CHEESE SANDWICH SPREAD

32 oz. finely shredded mild cheddar cheese
4 oz. jar diced pimento
½ c. pimento olives, diced
¾ c. chopped pecans
1 c. Hellmann's mayonnaise

Mix well and serve on whole wheat bread.

Frances Harris

SAUCY PARTY MEATBALLS

3 lbs. ground beef
1 c. milk
1 c. chopped onion
1 tsp. basil
2 beaten eggs
1 c. seasoned breadcrumbs
1 tbsp. chopped parsley
Salt/pepper to taste

Mix all ingredients together thoroughly. Form in small balls. Cook in hot skillet with 4 tablespoons of oil until all sides are browned. Drain on paper towels.

Sauce:
2 bottles chili sauce
1 small jar grape jelly

Cook these two ingredients in saucepan, stirring constantly until jelly is dissolved. Place meatballs in crock pot or warming dish and cover with sauce. Serve warm.

Genice Johnson

SAUSAGE BALLS

1 lb. hot sausage
1 pkg. buttermilk biscuit mix (approx. 3 cups)
2 c. grated sharp cheese (approx. 1 lb.)

Cut sausage into small pieces. Add cheese and mix (blend with hands or mixer). Roll in 1 inch balls. Freeze. Bake at 350 degrees, while frozen, for 25 minutes.

Christi Smith
(our daughter)

SMOKED OYSTER DIP

Mash 1 tin smoked oysters with oil and mix with 1 pint sour cream (I use low-fat). Stir well.

Season as follows, adjusting to taste:

¼ - ½ tsp. Worcestershire sauce
1/8 – ¼ tsp. Tabasco sauce
¼ tsp. salt
pinch of garlic salt
pinch of onion salt

Stir well. Refrigerate. Better if made several hours or day ahead. Serve with chips, crackers or vegetables (carrots, celery, etc.).

Meredith Henderson

SPINACH DIP

1 pkg. Knorr Swiss vegetable soup mix
2 green onions, chopped
6 oz. pkg. frozen shrimp, thawed and chopped
6-8 oz. can water chestnuts, drained and chopped
1 ½ c. mayonnaise
1 ½ c. sour cream
10 oz. pkg. chopped spinach, thawed and drained

Combine all ingredients until well mixed. Serve with bread or vegetables. May be served in hollowed-out bread "boat".

Bill Green

STUFFED ZUCCHINI

3 medium zucchini
2 tbsp. butter
1 c. chopped fresh mushrooms
2 tbsp. all-purpose flour
¼ c. grated Parmesan cheese
¼ tsp. dried oregano, crushed
1 c. (4 oz.) shredded Monterey Jack cheese
2 tbsp. chopped pimento

Cook whole zucchini in boiling salted water about 10 minutes, or until tender; drain. Cut in half length-wise. For zucchini curl, cut a thin horizontal slice from top of each zucchini half, cutting to - but not through- each end; roll up. Scoop out centers, leaving a ¼ inch shell; chop center portion and set aside.

Melt butter in a large skillet; sauté mushrooms about 3 minutes or until tender. Stir in flour, oregano; remove from heat. Stir in Monterey Jack cheese and pimento; stir in the reserved chopped zucchini. Heat mixture through.

Preheat broiler. Fill zucchini shells, using approximately ¼ cup filling for each. Sprinkle with Parmesan cheese. Broil several inches from source of heat for 3 to 5 minutes or until hot and bubbly.

Note: Stuffed zucchini may be assembled in advance, covered and refrigerated up to 4 hours. Broil for 5 - 7 minutes instead of 3 – 5.

Heidi & Carl Wallace

TIFFI'S MEXICAN CORN DIP

1-11 oz. can Mexicorn, drained
2 c. mild cheddar cheese, shredded
1 c. Hellmann's mayo
1-8 oz. sour cream
1- 4 oz. can chopped green chiles, drained

Mix all ingredients and put in refrigerator overnight. Serve with Fritos or Tortilla chips next day.

Tiffi Gentry

ZUCCHINI SQUARES

4 eggs, lightly beaten
½ c. vegetable oil
3 c. zucchini, sliced thin
1 c. Bisquick
½ c. onion, finely chopped
½ c. Parmesan cheese
1 tbsp. snipped parsley
½ tsp. salt
½ tsp. oregano
dash of pepper
1 clove garlic, finely chopped
½ tsp. Dijon mustard

Combine all ingredients. Pour into a greased 9x13 inch pan. Bake at 350 degrees for 25 to 35 minutes until lightly brown. Cut into squares and serve with more Parmesan cheese or sour cream.

Leah Karo

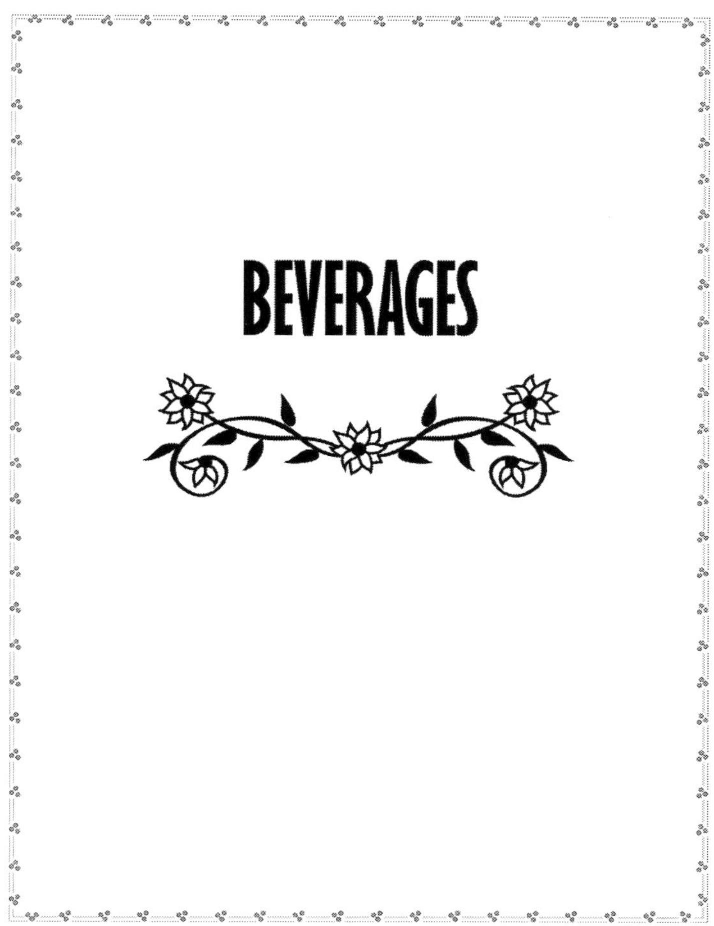

BEVERAGES

Notes...

EASY BOILED CUSTARD

5 c. milk
2/3 c. sugar
1 large box French Vanilla instant pudding

Bring to boil. Take off burner and wait until custard thickens.

Ready to serve – hot or cold!

Pam Greer

INSTANT SPICE TEA

1/2 c. instant tea with lemon or instant tea and pkg. of lemon mix
1 tsp. cinnamon
2 c. sugar
2 c. Tang
1 tsp. cloves
boiling water- 2 tbsp./cup

Peggy Mayes

PAT'S PUNCH

1 large can pineapple juice
1 large can unsweetened grapefruit juice
1 large can apple juice
1 liter bottle 7-Up

Pat Dunn

PERCOLATOR PUNCH

Pour in percolator:
4 ½ c. water
9 c. cranberry juice cocktail
9 c. unsweetened pineapple juice

Put in percolator basket:
1 c. brown sugar
½ tsp. salt
4 sticks cinnamon
4 ½ tsp. whole cloves

Perk and serve. Makes 30 cups.

Dorothy Ann McArthur

PUNCH

2 (6 oz.) cans frozen orange juice

2 (6 oz.) cans frozen lemonade

2 (46 oz.) cans red fruit punch

2 (1-liter) bottles ginger ale

Mix all above ingredients together. Recipe makes 5 quarts which equals 80 one-fourth cup servings.

Harriet Greer

SANDRA'S WASSAIL

2 qts. apple juice or cider
¼ c. sugar
2 sticks cinnamon
1 tsp. whole allspice
1 c. rum (optional)
1 pt. cranberry juice
1 tsp. aromatic bitters
1 small orange studded with whole cloves

Mix all ingredients and cook in crock pot on high for one hour then turn down to low for 4-8 hrs. May also leave in pot on stove on low and serve from pot. Put spices in spice bag or allow to float.

Sandra Shoemake

BREADS

Notes...

AUNT AMELIA'S CORN BREAD

2 c. corn meal, hot rise, self-rise
1 c. sugar
1 pkg. dry yeast
2 tbsp. Crisco
½ c. all purpose flour
1 tsp. salt
2 c. buttermilk

Spray loaf pan with Pam.
Melt Crisco in pan in 350 degree oven.

Mix remaining ingredients in a separate bowl and pour in loaf pan and stir. Bake at 350 degrees for 45 minutes. This recipe is for 1 loaf of corn bread.

Teresa & Chuck Fann

BANANA BREAD

½ c. shortening
1 c. sugar
2 eggs
¾ c. mashed ripe bananas
¾ tsp. soda
1 ¼ c. sifted all-purpose flour

Cream shortening and sugar until fluffy. Add eggs, one at a time, beating well after each. Stir in bananas. Sift together dry ingredients; add to banana mixture. Mix well. Pour into greased 9x9x2 inch pan. Bake at 350 degrees for 30-35 minutes.

Diane Cohn

BANANA NUT BREAD

2 c. self-rising flour
2 eggs
½ c. oleo, or 1 stick, melted
1 tsp. vanilla
1 c. sugar
1 tsp. soda
4 tbsp. buttermilk
2-3 large bananas, mashed well (1 c.)

Mix sugar and flour well. Melt oleo, beat eggs. Mix all ingredients together until smooth. Spray 2 medium size loaf pans or pyrex dish with Pam cooking spray. May use muffin pans. Makes 18. Cook slowly at 300 to 350 degrees until toothpick comes out clean.

(This recipe is from my mother, Ruby).

Sue Dodd Locke

BISCUITS

2 scant c. self-rising flour
½ pint whipping cream

When handling flour never pack into measuring cup. Handle lightly. Do not sift. Add the cream to flour. Mix well. Use a flour cloth and cloth cover for rolling pin. Dump the mixture on cloth with a sprinkling of self-rising flour. Knead dough a few minutes. Form a ball and start rolling. Starting from the center to outer edge, roll about ½ inch thick. Cut with regular size biscuit cutter. Place on aluminum (a must) cookie sheet. Cook immediately at 450 degrees on center rack in oven. These rise beautifully. Makes about 16 biscuits.

Caroline Jones Cross

BLUEBERRY- BANANA BREAD

½ c. shortening
2 large eggs
1 c. mashed ripe bananas
¼ tsp. salt
½ -1 c. blueberries,
(fresh or frozen)
1 c. sugar
1 tsp. vanilla
1 tsp. soda
½ c. uncooked oats
½ c. chopped nuts
1 ½ c. flour

Cream shortening and sugar; add eggs one at a time. Add vanilla; stir in mashed bananas. Sift soda, salt & flour together. Combine oats, blueberries and nuts with dry ingredients; then blend into creamed mixture, mixing only to moisten thoroughly. Pour into greased and floured 9x5 inch pan. I usually line pan first with foil, parchment or wax paper then grease and flour to be sure of getting out of pan easier.

Bake at 350 degrees for 50-55 minutes or until toothpick comes out clean. Cool in pan for 10 minutes before removing.

Viola Sanders
(Brent's Mom)

BROCCOLI CORNBREAD

2 boxes Jiffy cornbread mix
½ tsp. salt
1 onion, chopped
¾ c. cottage cheese
1 stick butter
¼ c. milk
1 box frozen broccoli
3 eggs
1 c. cheddar cheese

Combine all the above and bake at 350 degrees for 30-40 minutes.

Mary Trim Anderson

BROCCOLI & CHEESE CORNBREAD

1 box frozen chopped broccoli
(10 oz.) partially unthawed
2 tbsp. milk
1 stick melted butter
1 box Jiffy corn muffin mix
1 c. chopped onions
3 eggs, beaten
2 c. shredded cheddar cheese

Mix all ingredients together. Bake in 9 x 9 inch greased baking dish at 350 degrees for 45-50 minutes.

Michelle Johnson

BROWN & SERVE ROLLS

2 c. scalded milk
½ c. sugar
1 tsp. salt
2 eggs
½ c. warm water
½ c. shortening (oil)
2 cakes yeast

Dissolve yeast in water. Scald milk and add sugar and shortening. When cool (lukewarm), add yeast and enough flour to make a thick batter. Beat until batter is slick. Let rise to double. Add eggs and salt and beat well. Add enough flour to make a soft dough. Let rise to double and turn out on floured board. Roll and cut. Put in greased pan and let rise. Bake 25 minutes at 250 degrees. Do not let brown. Cool and store in plastic bags. Bake in hot oven until brown as desired.

(From Mrs. Robert N. Moore, Sr. – 1949)

Dorothy Rader

CORNBREAD

1 c. yellow corn meal
1 c. unsifted flour
2 tbsp. sugar
1 c. skim milk or low fat buttermilk
½ tsp. salt
1/3 c. allowed margarine
4 tsp. baking powder
½ c. (1/2 container) egg substitute

In large bowl combine corn meal, flour, sugar, baking powder and salt. Cut in margarine. Blend together milk and egg substitute. Stir into corn meal mixture. Beat for one minute. Pour into greased 8-inch square dish. Bake at 425 degrees for 20-25 minutes, or until done.

For Corn Muffins: Pour batter into 12 greased (with allowed fat) 3x1½ inch muffin pans. Bake at 400 degrees for 20-25 minutes.

For Corn Sticks: Pour batter into 24 well greased (with allowed fat) corn stick pans, filling each about 2/3 full. Bake at 425 degrees for 15-20 minutes. Yields 9. (From The Heart Network)

Charles Wilson

CORN LIGHT BREAD

3 c. Lily self-rising corn meal
1 c. sugar
1 c. sweet milk
1 c. Lily self-rising flour
2 c. buttermilk
¾ c. Wesson oil

Mix dry ingredients together. Mix buttermilk and sweet milk, add to dry ingredients and blend well. Add oil that has been heated in loaf pans to this mixture. Mix well.

Bake about 55 minutes or until done at 375 degrees. Yields 2 loaves.

Mary Lou Fox

DELICIOUS BANANA BREAD

1 c. self-rising flour
2 eggs
½ c. oil
1 tbsp. vanilla
½ c. crushed walnuts
1 c. Old Fashioned Quaker oats
1 c. sugar
½ c. raisins
4 large ripe bananas, mashed

Blend together the flour, sugar, oats, and set aside. Mix together the oil, eggs, vanilla, and bananas. Combine all ingredients, adding nuts and raisins.

Pour into greased loaf pans and bake at 375 degrees for 30 minutes, or until brown and inserted straw comes out clean. Makes 1 large loaf or 2 small loaves.

Betty Harvey

EASY BEER BREAD

3 c. flour
4 tsp. baking powder
butter
½ c. sugar
1 tsp. salt
12 oz. beer, room temp. (non-alcoholic brands work as well.)

Preheat oven to 350 degrees. In a large mixing bowl combine the flour, sugar, baking powder and salt. Add the beer and mix with a fork. Spread the dough in a 5x9x2 ½ inch bread pan and bake for 55 minutes. Brush the top of the loaf with butter when done.

Leah Karo

EASY ROLLS

1 pkg. yeast
2 ½ c. flour
2 tbsp. sugar
1 heaping tbsp. vegetable oil
1 c. warm water
1 tsp. salt
1 egg

Sift dry ingredients into a bowl. Add vegetable oil and cut in thoroughly. Dissolve yeast in warm water. Pour into the middle of flour. Add whole egg and start mixing from the middle – adding more flour to make a soft dough. Roll out on floured board. Cut into rolls and dip top of each roll into butter and fold over. Place in pan. Let rise in a warm place until double in size for about one hour. Bake in 450 degree oven.

Anna Kinnard Broome

HERBERT'S BAR-B-Q QUICK CORN LIGHT BREAD

2 c. Martha White self-rising meal
1 c. Martha White self-rising flour
1 c. sugar
3-4 c. fresh buttermilk

Combine the first three ingredients. Mix well and add buttermilk, approximately 1 qt… and sometimes a little less, depending on the freshness of the milk. Batter should be the consistency of cake batter. Be sure it is not too thick or stiff because it will be crumbly and not waxy inside. Spray pan or skillet with non-stick cooking spray. Put small egg- size Crisco in cooking container and heat in preheated oven at 350 degrees for a few minutes until hot. Pour batter into loaf pan or skillet approximately ½ to 2/3 full. Bake at 350 degrees for 30 minutes and then turn back to 300 degrees for 30 minutes or until golden brown. It may take 5-10 minutes longer depending on your oven. Cool on wire rack approximately 5 minutes before cutting to serve.

(continued next page)

(This is the recipe that I used at Herbert's Bar-B-Q Restaurant from October 11, 1986 until it closed. Several people have asked for this recipe and I'm happy to share it now since the restaurant has been closed. It was given to me by my mother, Mrs. Gene Givens from Hillsboro – now "Leipers Fork".)

Carolyn Dodson

SPOON ROLLS

1 pkg. dry yeast, dissolved
¼ c. sugar
1 egg, beaten
2 c. very warm water (use some of this to dissolve yeast).
1 ½ sticks margarine, melted
4 c. self-rising flour

Melt margarine. Mix sugar and water in large mixing bowl. Add beaten egg, then dissolved yeast. Add flour. Stir until well mixed. Place in air-tight bowl in refrigerator. It will keep about a week.

To cook, drop by spoonfuls into greased muffin tins. Bake at 350 degrees 15-20 minutes or until browned. Makes 2 dozen.

This recipe came from the old Satsuma Tea Room in Nashville.

Gwen King

STRAWBERRY BREAD

3 c. flour
3 tsp. cinnamon
1 c. chopped pecans
4 eggs, beaten
2 pkgs. (10 oz.) frozen
  strawberries (thawed)
2 c. sugar
1 tsp. soda
1 tsp. salt
1 ¼ c. oil

Mix ingredients. Grease and flour 2 pans. Bake at 325 degrees for 1 hour. Makes 2 loaves.

Janice Green

VIDALIA ONION CUSTARD BREAD

1 large Vidalia or sweet onion,
  halved and sliced
1 egg
¾ c. shredded cheddar
  cheese, divided
3 tbsp. butter, divided
1 ¾ c. flour
1 ¼ c. milk
1 tsp. poppy seeds

In a large skillet, cook onion in 2 tbsp. butter over medium-low heat, until very tender and lightly browned. Beat egg and add milk. Slowly mix into flour, stirring just until moistened. Set aside 2 tbsp. onion mixture and fold remaining mixture into batter. Fold in ½ cup cheese. Pour into greased 9 inch pie plate.

Top with remaining cheese and reserved onion. Sprinkle with poppy seeds. Melt remaining butter and drizzle over the top. Bake at 400 degrees for 30-35 minutes until knife comes out clean. Cool for 10 minutes, serve warm. Serves 8-10.

Debbie Connell

BREAKFAST

Notes...

BREAKFAST EGG & SAUSAGE

6 beaten eggs
6 slices white bread, cubed
2 c. milk
1 c. grated cheddar cheese
1 tsp. salt
1 tbsp. dry mustard
1 lb. bulk sausage

Cook meat and drain off grease. Mix eggs, salt, mustard and milk. Add cubed bread. Stir together. Add meat and cheese and refrigerate overnight.

Bake in a 9x13 inch greased pan at 350 degrees for 45 minutes.

Elva Beard

BREAKFAST SAUSAGE CASSEROLE

1 lb. mild sausage
½ c. chopped green pepper
6 eggs
1 c. chopped onion
½ c. chopped red pepper
1 ½ c. milk
6 slices bread – recommend sourdough French
1 c. shredded sharp cheddar cheese

Brown sausage in skillet, then add onion and pepper, cooking until done. Drain well and pat with paper towels. Cube bread and place in greased casserole dish. Place sausage and pepper mix on top of bread. Whip eggs with milk, and pour on top of mix – pressing down with forks so bread will become moist. Top with cheese and place in refrigerator. THIS CAN BE PREPARED THE AFTERNOON BEFORE SERVING.

Bake at 375 degrees for 40 to 45 minutes. Best to check at about 30 minutes and monitor.

(This is a Bacon family breakfast favorite.)

Nell Bacon

BRUNCH CASSEROLE

8 slices bread – crust removed
7 eggs
½ lb. sharp grated cheddar cheese
1 lb. hot sausage – browned & crumbled
1 lb. mild sausage – browned & crumbled
2 ¾ c. milk
1 tbsp. dry mustard
1 tsp. salt

Cut bread into cubes. Place half in buttered 13 x 9 inch casserole dish. Layer half of the cheese and half of the sausage on top of bread. Repeat layers. Beat eggs, milk, mustard and salt. Pour over layer. Cover and chill overnight. Bake at 350 degrees for 45 minutes. Let stand a few minutes before serving. Serves 8.

Katherine Whitley

BRUNCH EGG CASSEROLE

6 slices bread, cubed
8 eggs, beaten
4 c. milk
1 tsp. prepared mustard
1/8 tsp. pepper
8 oz. cheddar cheese, shredded
1 tsp. salt
¼ tsp. onion powder

Spread bread cubes into bottom of 13 x 8 x 1 inch baking dish. Sprinkle cheddar cheese over bread. Mix together all remaining ingredients. Pour over bread-cheese mixture.

Bake at 325 degrees until egg mixture is set - about 40-45 minutes. Crisp cook and crumble 10 slices of bacon and sprinkle over casserole during last 10 minutes of cooking time (optional). Serves 10.

Carolyn White

CINNAMON APPLES

8 medium size apples
1 c. water
Dash salt
1 ¾ oz. cinnamon candies
1 c. sugar
Red food coloring (optional)

Peel and core apples. Combine sugar, water, salt & cinnamon candies. Boil until candies dissolve and mixture is syrupy. Gently simmer apples – 3 or 4 at a time in syrup until Christmas red. Drain and put in dish (whole, halved, or sliced). Cool before serving.

Preferred varieties: Washington State, Rome Beauty, Gold Delicious, or Winesap.

Margaret Hooper

FRENCH TOAST

1 ½ c. brown sugar
¼ c. + 2 tablespoons light karo
¾ c. margarine

Combine together in saucepan and bring to boil. Cook 5 minutes and pour into 9 x 13 inch pan. Lay 10 thick slices of French bread on mixture.

.

COMBINE:
4 – 6 eggs
1 tsp. vanilla
2 ½ c. milk
¼ tsp. salt

Pour over bread, cover, and refrigerate overnight. Preheat oven to 350 degrees. Melt ¼ cup margarine and pour over bread. Combine 3 tablespoons sugar and 1 ½ teaspoons cinnamon and sprinkle over bread. Bake 45–50 minutes. Serve hot.

Cassie Olson

GRIT CASSEROLE

Cook 1 cup of grits according to directions.

1 stick butter, melted
1 roll of garlic-cheese or use processed cheese and garlic powder to taste
2 eggs
milk

Combine first 2 ingredients and cool. Beat 2 eggs well and add milk to make 1 cup. Mix all together. Pour into casserole and sprinkle with bread crumbs.

Bake at 350 degrees for 1 hour without cover. Serves 10.

Lois Hall

GRITS CASSEROLE

1 c. grits
1 stick butter
4 garlic cloves (crushed with garlic press)
2 eggs
1 small box Velvetta cheese
Ritz crackers

Cook grits as directed on box. Melt butter in skillet and add garlic. Cook 1 minute. Beat eggs. Add the butter mixture and eggs to grits. Bake at 350 degrees for 35 minutes. Add topping of crushed Ritz crackers, grated cheddar cheese and butter pieces. Bake 5 minutes more.

Sue Jeter

HEART HEALTHY MUFFINS

1 c. raw oats
1 c. unbleached all-purpose flour
3 egg whites
¾ c. non-fat plain yogurt
2 tbsp. molasses
½ c. raisins
½ c. pecans
½ c. slivered almonds
1 ½ tsp. baking soda
1 tsp. baking powder
½ tsp. salt
1/3 c. applesauce
¼ c. brown sugar
¾ c. chopped dates (not sugared kind)
½ c. walnuts

Combine dry ingredients and stir well. In another bowl combine rest of ingredients. Whisk until smooth and well blended. Add dry ingredients. Do not over-mix. Spray muffin tin with nonstick spray. Spoon about ¼ c. batter into each muffin cup, filling cup almost full. Bake at 400 degrees for about 15 minutes. Yummy!

Jan Rains

HOLIDAY BREAKFAST CASSEROLE

1 cup brown sugar, packed
2 tbsp. corn syrup
1 ½ c. milk
1 loaf French bread
(cut into thick slices)
½ c. butter
5 eggs
1 tsp. vanilla extract

In a medium sauce pan over medium heat, mix and melt brown sugar, butter and corn syrup. Spray a baking dish with non-stick vegetable oil and fill with butter mixture. Mix eggs, milk and vanilla. Arrange bread slices in baking dish. Pour egg mixture over bread; don't miss any area. Use all the mixture - any extra will be soaked up by the bread. Cover dish and refrigerate overnight. The next morning, simply uncover and slip into a 350 degree oven for 30 minutes, then serve. A big hit with kids!

Carolyn Dodson

I'M SO BLUEBERRY COFFEECAKE

2 c. self-rising flour
¾ c. sugar
2 c. blueberries
¼ c. butter
1 egg
½ c. milk

Grease and flour an 8 inch square pan. Cream ¼ cup of butter and beat in ¾ cup of sugar. Add the egg and milk and beat well. Gradually add the 2 cups flour. Fold the blueberries into the batter. Pour batter into prepared pan.

CRUMB TOPPING:
¼ c. all purpose flour
½ tsp. cinnamon
½ c. sugar
¼ c. butter

Mix sugar, flour and cinnamon. Cut in butter until mixture makes coarse crumbs. Sprinkle over batter. Bake at 350 degrees for about 35 minutes or until a toothpick inserted in the center comes out clean (I find that I have to cook this closer to 40 minutes).

Lynn Babcock

MOM'S WAFFLES

2 c. flour – sifted
3 eggs
4 tbsp. melted butter
2 tsp. sugar
1 ¼ c. milk

Mix flour, sugar, egg yolks, milk and butter. Beat egg whites until stiff – then fold in mixture. Cook in greased waffle iron until golden brown

SYRUP:
1 c. water
maple flavoring
2 c. sugar

Boil until sugar is melted. Pour over waffle. GOOD!

Bobbye Noland

NIGHT BEFORE BREAKFAST CASSEROLE

1 lb. cooked sausage
1 c. half and half
½ tsp. dry mustard
1 bag sour dough croutons (Kroger)
5 eggs
2 c. cheddar cheese (grated)
dash of salt and pepper

Pour croutons in bottom of 9 x 13 inch baking dish. Sprinkle sausage around. Cover with cheddar cheese. Mix remaining ingredients and pour on top. Wrap in aluminum foil and refrigerate overnight.

In morning, preheat oven to 350 degrees and bake casserole in oven for 50 minutes to 1 hour. Center will be firm and casserole browned.

Danelle Pate

PECAN PIE MUFFINS

1 c. light brown sugar
2 eggs
1 c. pecans
½ c. all purpose flour
2/3 c. melted butter (salted)

Preheat over to 350 degrees. Mix all ingredients together with wooden spoon. Pour in greased mini-muffin pans 2/3 full. Bake 12 to 15 minutes. Wonderful dish for a brunch!

Genice Johnson

CASSEROLES & VEGETABLES

Notes...

ASPARAGUS ALMOND CASSEROLE

STEP #1:
Mix together 3 tbsp. flour, 4 tbsp. butter (1/2 stick) and ½ c. warm milk. Add 1 glass jar Old English cheese spread and salt and pepper to taste.
STEP #2:
1 ½ c. finely crumbled Ritz cracker crumbs
½ cup melted butter (1 stick)
STEP #3:
2 average size cans green asparagus spears
½ c. sliced almonds

In casserole dish, place ½ of the buttered crumbs on the bottom. Then add asparagus spears (drained). Next layer, add almonds. Top with cheese spread mixture and finish with remainder of buttered crumbs. Sprinkle with paprika.
Bake at 450 degrees for 12 minutes. Serves 6 to 8.

Harry Lee Billington

BROCCOLI CASSEROLE

1 pkg. frozen broccoli (16 oz.)
1 can cream of mushroom soup
Velveeta cheese slices
1 tube Ritz crackers, crushed
Butter pats

Break broccoli apart and place in 9 x 9 inch baking dish. (do not thaw.) Cover with mushroom soup, then add cheese slices. Top with crushed cracker crumbs and pats of butter. Bake at 350 degrees for 60 minutes.

Billie Ruth Wade

BROCCOLI, HAM & CHEESE CASSEROLE

Bread crumbs
1 head fresh broccoli –or-
  1 pkg. frozen broccoli
2 thick slices ham-cut in chunks
1 small jar Cheez-Whiz
¼ c. milk

Cook broccoli for 5 minutes in boiling unsalted water. In a small pan melt cheese with milk. Put broccoli in a baking dish. Add ham chunks on top of broccoli. Pour cheese sauce on top of broccoli and ham. Top with bread crumbs and bake at 350 degrees until bread crumbs are browned.

Margaret Gilham

CATHERINE'S ASPARAGUS PARISIENNE

2 lbs. fresh asparagus
2 c. sour cream
black pepper to taste
¼ lb. Parmesan cheese
  (grated)
4 tbsp. butter

Cook asparagus in salted water until just tender. Drain. Layer asparagus and cheese several times in a 9 inch square casserole dish, ending with a layer of asparagus. Dot with butter. Season sour cream with pepper and cover top layer. Sprinkle with breadcrumbs and paprika.

Bake at 350 degrees for 30 minutes – or until top is brown. Oooh, so good!

Catherine Williams

CHICKEN CASSEROLE

2 c. chopped cooked chicken
½ c. mayonnaise
1 can cream of chicken soup
½ c. slivered almonds
1 c. chopped celery
1 tsp. chopped onion
2 hard boiled eggs, sliced

Mix all ingredients and top with buttered bread crumbs. Bake at 350 degrees until bubbly.

Charles & Carol Bond

CHICKEN CASSEROLE

½ c. (1 stick) butter or margarine
1 c. chopped onion
3 c. diced, cooked chicken breasts
1 can sliced mushrooms, (4 oz.), with liquid
1 c. chopped celery
½ c. chopped green pepper
1 jar chopped pimento (4 oz.)
4 tbsp. flour
3 c. cooked rice
1 ½ c. chicken broth
1 ½ tsp. salt – more to taste
1 can evap. milk (12 oz.)
1 tbsp. curry powder
½ c. slivered almonds, toasted

Melt butter in large saucepan. Add onion and cook until transparent. Blend in flour. Add broth, milk, curry powder and salt. Cook over low heat until thickened. Add rice, chicken, celery, mushrooms, pimento and green peppers. Mix well. Pour into buttered casserole dish. Bake at 350 degrees for 30 minutes. Top with slivered almonds

Dot Ladd

CHICKEN CASSEROLE

5 c. cooked, chopped chicken breasts
¼ c. chopped onion
1 can water chestnuts
2 tbsp. lemon juice
2 -10 oz. cans cream of chicken soup
2 c. chopped celery
1 sm. jar pimentos
1 sm. jar mushrooms
2/3 c. Hellmann's mayo
crushed Ritz crackers

Mix all ingredients together. Put in 9 x 13 inch baking dish. Top with crushed crackers and dot with pats of butter. Bake at 350 degrees for 30 to 45 minutes or until bubbly.

Carrie Ozburn

CHICKEN CASSEROLE

2 c. sliced cooked chicken
1 can cream of chicken soup
1 tsp. lemon juice
2 tbsp. melted butter
¼ c. grated cheese
½ c. mayonnaise
¼ c. chicken broth (optional)
1 c. rice

Boil rice until done. Add chicken, soup, lemon juice, butter, grated cheese, mayonnaise and chicken broth. Mix together and pour into casserole dish. Bake at 350 degrees for 30 to 40 minutes.

Isabel Pritchett

CHICKEN & ASPARAGUS CASSEROLE

6 whole chicken breasts
1 medium onion chopped
½ c. butter
1 can cream of mushroom soup
1 can cream of chicken soup
1 can mushrooms (8oz.)
2 cans green-tipped asparagus
½ lb. ex. sharp cheese, grated
¼ tsp. Tabasco sauce
2 tsp. Soy sauce
1 tsp. salt & ½ tsp. pepper
1 tsp. Accent
2 tbsp. pimento chopped
1- 5-1/3 oz. can Pet milk
½ c. slivered almonds

Drain canned mushrooms and asparagus. Boil chicken breasts in water seasoned with salt and pepper until tender. Cool, debone and tear into bite size pieces. Saute onions in butter and add remaining ingredients except asparagus and almonds. Simmer on low heat until cheese melts.

Place a layer of chicken into a large casserole dish.

Add asparagus for next layer.

.
Cover with a layer of sauce.

Repeat layers and top with slivered almonds.

.
Bake at 350 degrees until bubbly. Do not add liquid, even if it looks dry. Serves 12.

Freezes well.

Ann Conway

CHICKEN & RICE CASSEROLE

3 c. diced cooked chicken
1 can cream of mushroom soup, undiluted
¾ c. mayonnaise
1 c. diced celery
1 tbsp. grated onion
3 tbsp. butter melted
4 tbsp. chopped pimento
1 tbsp. lemon juice
2 c. cooked rice (cooked in chicken broth)
1 jar mushrooms (14 oz.), drained
1 c. Ritz cracker crumbs
1 c. slivered almonds

Mix together all ingredients except almonds, cracker crumbs and melted butter. Place in baking dish. Top with cracker crumbs mixed with butter and almonds on top of cracker crumbs. Bake 30 to 40 minutes at 350 degrees.

Mary Lou Fox

CHICKEN & YELLOW RICE CASSEROLE

1 lb. boneless chicken, cut into bite size pieces
1 c. yellow rice
1 can mushroom soup (10 oz. size)
1 c. milk
½ stick butter
¾ c. grated cheese
salt & pepper to taste

Put uncooked rice in bottom of casserole. Add raw chicken on top of rice. Add salt and pepper, mushroom soup and milk to chicken and rice. Add butter and sprinkle with cheese.

Bake at 350 degrees for 1 hour.

Katherine Hood

EASY RICE CASSEROLE

1 c. raw rice
1 stick butter
1 small can sliced mushrooms, drained
1 can chicken broth
2 tbsp. wild rice
1 can French onion soup
1 small can sliced water chestnuts, drained

Mix all ingredients together in greased casserole dish. Cover and bake at 350 degrees for 1 hour. Serves 5.

Jo Ann Irwin

ENCHILADA CASSEROLE

1 lb. ground chuck
½ cup chunky (mild or medium) Salsa
1 pkg. flour tortillas
1 can mild enchilada sauce
1 can cream of chicken soup
1 lb. grated cheddar cheese

Brown ground chuck (drain fat). Add enchilada sauce, salsa, cream of chicken soup and mix well.

Layer as follows in a 9 x 13 inch baking dish:

1. Flour tortillas
2. Meat sauce mixture
3. Small amount of the cheese
4. Repeat # 1,2, & 3 – ending with tortillas

Bake at 350 degrees until golden brown (approximately 1 hour). Remove from oven, top with another layer of cheese. Put back in oven just until cheese melts. Serve with lettuce, cream cheese and salsa. Also good with Mexican rice.

Karla Landrum

HASH BROWN CASSEROLE

2 lb. bag shredded hash brown potatoes
1 can cream of chicken soup
½ c. melted margarine
1 small container sour cream
¾ c. chopped onions
¾ c. cheddar cheese
salt & pepper to taste

Mix all ingredients together and bake at 350 degrees for 45 minutes.

Mary Alice Trice

HOT BROWN CASSEROLE

Layer in a 2-1/2 qt. casserole dish (as follows):

1. layer of toast
2. layer of asparagus or broccoli
3. layer of cooked chicken pieces or ham pieces
4. layer of crumbled cooked bacon

Top with cheese sauce (as follows):
1 can cheddar cheese soup mixed with ½ - 1 can milk
½ lb. Velveeta cheese, cubed
salt/pepper to taste
sprinkle paprika on top

Bake at 350 degrees 30 minutes or until golden brown. Serves 2-4.

Judy Eggleston

PEA CASSEROLE

1 medium onion, sliced
½ stick butter
1 can mushroom soup
1 small can sliced mushrooms, drained
½ c. slivered almonds
½ c. water chestnuts
1 tbsp. Worcestershire sauce
2 – 17 oz cans small green peas, drained
salt & pepper to taste

Saute onion in butter until tender. Combine next 6 ingredients with cooked onion and butter. Fold in peas and place in buttered casserole dish. Sprinkle with paprika.

Bake at 350 degrees for 15 minutes.

Ruby Covington

PINEAPPLE CASSEROLE

½ c. butter
¼ large loaf soft bread, cubed
1 c. brown sugar, packed
#2 can crushed pineapple

Melt butter and add brown sugar. Place in a greased casserole dish, a layer of cubed bread, a layer of pineapple, and a layer of butter/sugar sauce.

Repeat layers and bake at 325 degrees for one hour.

Adair Shanks

PINEAPPLE & CHEESE CASSEROLE

2 large cans chunk pineapple (drained- save juice)
1 ½ c. sugar
6 tbsp. flour
6 tbsp. pineapple juice
2 c. grated cheddar cheese
3 c. crushed Ritz crackers
1 stick margarine, melted

Mix flour and sugar together. Add in pineapple, juice and cheese. Place in a long casserole dish . Top with crushed crackers and melted butter.

Bake at 350 degrees for 30 minutes

Debbie Moody

POTATO CHEESE CASSEROLE

Boil 6 medium potatoes. Cool, peel, and cut in cubes.

ADD:

1 c. sour cream
2 tbsp. green onion, chopped
1 c. grated cheddar cheese
2 c. cottage cheese
1 tsp. salt
2 tsp. sugar

Place in 1 ½ qt. baking dish. Top with grated cheese and bake at 350 degrees for 45 minutes. Serves 10-12.

Vickie McArthur
(our daughter)

SAUSAGE BEEF CASSEROLE

1 lb. sweet Italian sausages
1 large onion sliced
4 medium potatoes, peeled and cut into qtrs.
2 cans red kidney beans, drained
2 medium garlic cloves, minced
½ tsp. salt
1 lb. beef chuck cut into 1" cubes (or ground beef)
2 medium green peppers, cut into eighths
1 tsp. basil
¼ tsp. pepper
2 beef bouillon cubes in 1 c. boiling water

Brown sausages well and cut each link into bite size pieces and place into 3 qt. casserole. Drain fat from skillet, reserving 2 tbsp. Brown beef and put into casserole. Then brown onion and garlic and place in casserole. Put beans into casserole, then potatoes and green peppers. Sprinkle with seasonings and mix. Add bouillon, cover and bake at 350 degrees for 1 hour and 15 minutes (or until tender). Serve with warm bread and tossed salad.

Sandra Shoemake

SOUR CREAM CHICKEN CASSEROLE

1/4 c. melted butter
3 whole chicken breasts (cooked and cut into bite size pieces)
1 (10 oz.) can cream of chicken soup, undiluted
1 c. crushed cracker crumbs
1 (8 oz.) container sour cream
¼ c. chicken broth

Combine butter and cracker crumbs; spoon ½ the crumbs into a 2 quart casserole. Cover with chicken. Combine sour cream, soup and broth; pour over chicken. Top with remaining cracker crumbs. Bake at 350 degrees for 20 to 25 minutes.

- If you want a little zest you can use French onion sour cream dip in place of plain sour cream.

Sue Pratt

SPINACH CASSEROLE

2 pkgs. chopped frozen spinach
1 c. sour cream
1 tbsp. apple cider vinegar
4 tbsp. butter or margarine
1 roll jalapeno cheese (6 oz.)

Cook spinach and drain well. Melt butter in casserole dish. Mix all ingredients together and pour into casserole dish. Mix well with butter.

Bake at 325 degrees for 30 to 40 minutes. Delicious!!

Ann Lee

SQUASH CASSEROLE

3 lbs. yellow or
 zucchini squash, or both
3 eggs, beaten
1 can cream of mushroom
 or cream of chicken soup
1 c. shredded cheese
1 chopped onion (optional)
¼ c. butter
salt to taste
¾ tsp. black pepper
cracker crumbs or stuffing
 mix for topping

Cook squash and onion until tender. Drain well. Add butter, eggs and remaining ingredients, mix well. Place in buttered casserole dish and top with cracker crumbs or stuffing mix or mix with the other ingredients. Top with shredded cheese or sprinkle cheese on top after dish is removed from oven. Bake at 350 degrees 30-45 minutes.

Gilda Bowman

SWISS VEGGIE CASSEROLE

1 ½ c. sliced yellow squash
1 ½ c. chopped broccoli -1" pieces
½ c. grated Swiss cheese
¼ c. grated Parmesan cheese
½ c. butter
1 egg
¼ c. milk
1 tsp. dry mustard
1 tsp. salt

Sauté veggies in butter until they can be pierced with a fork. In large bowl beat egg, stir in milk, salt, mustard and cheese. Place veggies in 1 quart casserole. Cover with above mixture.

Bake uncovered at 300 degrees for 20 minutes or until thoroughly cooked.

Polly McFarlin

VEG-ALL CASSEROLE

½ large bell pepper, chopped
1 onion chopped
¾ c. mayonnaise
1 can cream of chicken soup
2 cans Veg-all, drained
1 can sliced water chestnuts, (drained)
1 can shoepeg corn, drained

Mix all ingredients together. Pour in 9 x 13 inch Pyrex dish.

Top with crushed Ritz crackers and ¾ stick butter or margarine cut in pieces over crackers.

Bake at 350 degrees for 30 to 35 minutes

Debbie Bennett

ZUCCHINI CASSEROLE

4 -6" long zucchini, sliced
1 large onion, chopped
2 tbsp. butter
½ tsp. salt
1/8 tsp. Oregano
1 tsp. parsley
½ c. grated cheddar cheese
Parmesan cheese
1 carton cottage cheese
2 eggs, beaten
2 tbsp. salad dressing
2 tbsp. flour
2 tsp. Soy sauce
1 – 1 lb can tomatoes
¼ c. cracker crumbs

Slice squash and onion and sauté in butter and seasonings. Mix together cottage cheese, beaten eggs, salad dressing, flour and parsley.

Layer as follows in buttered casserole dish:

½ Squash mixture

½ Cottage cheese mixture

All tomatoes

All of cheddar cheese

Repeat steps #1 & #2

Top with cracker crumbs and parmesan cheese.

Bake at 400 degrees for approximately 1 hour.

Mary Anne Bush

AU GRATIN POTATOES

8 large potatoes
¼ c. finely chopped onion
¼ c. butter
¼ c. flour
4 c. milk
1 tsp. salt
¼ tsp. hot pepper sauce
¼ tsp. marjoram
2 c. shredded cheddar cheese

Cook unpeeled potatoes in a saucepan covered with water until tender. Drain, peel and cube. Saute onion in butter in sauce pan. Add flour, mix well. Remove from heat. Stir in milk gradually. Cook over medium heat until thickened, stirring constantly. Add seasonings and cheese; stir until cheese melts. Mix in potatoes.

Pour into casserole dish and bake at 350 degrees for 25 minutes. Garnish with paprika and parsley.

Catherine L. Grice

CALIFORNIA POTATOES

6-7 large Idaho potatoes
1 medium onion, finely chopped
1 c. sour cream
½ lb. grated cheese
1 can cream of chicken soup
1 can cream of mushroom soup

Peel and slice potatoes very thin, cooking in small amount of water for 5 minutes. Drain. Mix soup and sour cream for sauce. Using a 13 x 9 x 2 inch casserole dish, layer half the potatoes, half the onions, and half the sauce. Make 2 layers of each, ending with cheese. Bake at 350 degrees for 1 hour.

Carolyn Carter

CHEESE SCALLOPED CORN

2 eggs, beaten
2/3 c. milk
1 c. cracker crumbs (about 24)
1 c. cheddar cheese
1/8 tsp. pepper
2 cans cream style corn (15 oz.)
½ c. chopped onion
½ c. bell pepper
¼ tsp. salt

Stir all ingredients together and bake uncovered in 2 qt. dish at 350 degrees for about 50 minutes. So good!

Millie Fly

FAVORITE BAKED BEANS

2 cans pork & beans (16 oz.)
1 can green lima beans (16 oz.)
1 can kidney beans (16 oz.)
3 tbsp. mustard
3-4 dashes Tabasco sauce
1/8 tsp. garlic powder
1 lb. bacon, cut up
1 large onion, chopped
½ of 1 lb. box brown sugar
1/3 c. ketchup
1 tsp. Worcestershire sauce
salt and pepper

Combine drained beans in casserole dish and set aside. Brown bacon, drain and reserve drippings. Brown onion in drippings and drain. Mix bacon, onions, and all other ingredients with beans.

Bake uncovered at 400 degrees for about 1 hour. Can freeze after cooking.

Libby Marley

MAMA WATT'S SPANISH RICE

1 c. rice
5 hot peppers
½ c. large onion chopped to ½" by ¼"
1 tsp. parsley flakes
4 slices bacon cut across width to ¼" strips
2 cans fine tomatoes (15 oz.)
½ tsp. garlic powder
salt and pepper

Boil 1 cup rice per directions; let cool; fry bacon and onion; combine with remaining ingredients. Bake in moderate oven (350 degrees) for 30 minutes or more. Remove peppers and serve.

In memory of my cousin, Olin.

Debbie Clark

MUSHROOMS & RICE

1 stick butter, melted
1 can consommé
1 c. rice
1 medium onion, chopped
1 can beef broth
1 jar sliced mushrooms

Saute onion in butter. Mix with other ingredients and place in casserole dish. Bake at 350 degrees for 1 hour. Enjoy!

Betty Pratt

PEAS & MUSHROOMS

1 can tiny peas (reserve liquid)
1 can mushrooms
2 tbsp. butter
2 tbsp. flour

Rub skillet with garlic and sauté mushrooms with butter. Remove mushrooms with slotted spoon. Add flour to juice in skillet. Stir and cook until bubbly. Combine and stir in slowly:

1/3 c. liquid from peas
1/3 c. cream (Half & Half)
Season with salt and pepper to taste

When sauce is smooth and boiling add the peas and mushrooms. Cover and simmer for a few minutes.

Gracy Henry

STUFFED SQUASH

4 yellow summer squash
½ pkg. bacon
1 onion, finely chopped
3 tbsp. bread crumbs
butter

Boil squash in salted water for 20 minutes. Drain and run cold water over squash. Fry ½ package bacon and crumble. Saute onion in bacon grease. Cut squash in half lengthwise and scoop out insides. Mix onion, crumbled bacon, 3 tbsp. bread crumbs and insides of squash. Fill squash up with mixture and place a pat of butter on each squash. Bake at 325 degrees for 30 minutes.

Irby Bright

SWEET POTATO PUDDING

3 large sweet potatoes
4 tsp. vanilla
sprinkle of plain flour
½ pt. Half & Half
1 1/3 c. sugar (or to taste)
¾ stick butter
2 pt. heavy cream
Dash salt

Grate potatoes. Add cream, half & half, salt, sugar, vanilla and flour. Stir well. Pout into buttered baking dish. Microwave for 10 minutes. Remove and stir and dot with ¾ stick butter. Return to microwave and cook 20 minutes. Remove, stir and cook another 20 minutes. Brown in conventional oven.

Kate Crutcher

FISH & SEAFOOD

Notes...

BAKED SALMON & TARTER SAUCE

2 lb. filet of salmon
1 tsp. salt
1 tsp. freshly ground black pepper
¼ tsp. red pepper
juice of one lemon
1 tbsp. olive oil
1tbsp. dill
½ tsp. minced garlic (on each side)
 fresh garlic can be used
white wine

Mix all spices together and generously sprinkle on salmon. Place salmon in enamel baking pan with 1 tablespoon olive oil. Partially cover filet with at least one cup of white wine (the kind that is good enough to drink!). Let marinate for 2 to 4 hours in refrigerator. Remove from refrigerator for at least 1 hour prior to cooking.

Preheat oven to 450 degrees then turn oven up to broil. Place filet in oven and cook in marinade for 12 minutes (cook 1 minute longer for each extra pound of fish) depending on preferred doneness. Remove from oven and sprinkle with 1 tbsp. dill (dried or fresh). Serve immediately

TARTER SAUCE

1 c. Hellmann's light mayonnaise
2 tbsp. freshly grated onion
2 tbsp. fresh or dried dill
½ c. Hidden Valley ranch dressing
juice of ½ lemon
1 tsp. dried minced garlic
1 tbsp. Dijon mustard
1 tsp. Worcestershire sauce
2 tbsp. dill pickle relish
salt/pepper to taste

Mix well, chill and serve.

Gertrude Caldwell

BROILED TALAPIA w/BUTTERCREAM SAUCE

4 Talapia filets (or other white fish)
Rice, preferably Uncle Bens' converted
1 large onion- quartered
1/3 green bell pepper-sliced thin strips
1/3 yellow bell pepper-sliced thin strips
1/3 red bell pepper-sliced thin strips
1 mushroom-sliced thinly
2 cups broccoli crowns
1 small zucchini squash - peeled, sliced thin, then quartered
1 small carton heavy whipping cream
1 small can pineapple chunks
3 tbsp. butter or oleo
lemon juice
olive oil
salt
pepper
paprika
garlic powder
parsley (fresh is best) chopped
½ cup Italian dressing
1 tbsp. brandy or red wine

DIRECTIONS:

Melt butter in microwave. Pour whipping cream in a mixing bowl. Add melted butter and brandy to cream. Mix thoroughly until stiff peaks form. Cover and chill in refrigerator. Wash fish and pat dry. Marinate fish in lemon juice for 10 minutes. While fish is marinating, combine vegetables and Italian dressing in a bowl. Add salt/pepper to taste and toss. Place fish in a well greased pan and sprinkle with salt, pepper, paprika, garlic powder and parsley. Place on lowest rack in oven and turn to broil. Cook rice according to directions on box. In a deep, non stick skillet or wok, cook vegetables until done (not too soft). Add pineapple to vegetables last minutes of cooking. When fish is done (flakes easily) remove from oven. On a plate, place fish on a bed of rice. Spoon out 1-2 tablespoons of butter-cream on top of fish. Add veggies on side. Serve with choice of bread. (I prefer yeast rolls topped with honey butter.)

Serves 4. ENJOY! Prepare yourself for compliments!

Sherri Stone

CHILI-LIME FISH FILLET

2 tbsp. olive oil
1 bunch basil, coarsely chopped
1 Thai or serrano chile pepper
(any hot pepper will work)
1 lb. fish filet (Red Snapper, Tilapia, etc)
1 lime

Heat oil in large skillet over medium heat. Add basil and pepper. Cook one minute then remove from pan and set aside. Add fish to pan. Squeeze lime over fish and sprinkle with salt and pepper to taste. Cover and cook 5 minutes. Turn on other side and cook for 3 minutes. Serves four.

Ginger Houston

COMPANY SHRIMP CASSEROLE

1 ½ lbs. cooked, cleaned shrimp
2 cups cooked rice
1 cup grated sharp cheese
1 can mushroom soup
½ cup chopped green pepper
½ cup green onions, chopped
½ cup chopped celery
1 stick butter
4 lemons, thinly sliced

Mix first 4 ingredients. Saute green peppers, green onions and celery in butter. Add to shrimp mixture. Put in 9 x 13 inch baking dish that has been sprayed with cooking spray. Cover with sliced lemons. Cover with foil.

Bake at 375 degrees for 20 minutes. May be frozen ahead.

Mrs. Jimmy "Pug" Akin

COMPANY SHRIMP CASSEROLE

½ cup celery, chopped
½ cup green pepper, chopped
2 tbsp. butter
2 cups cooked rice
dash of red pepper
Dry sherry to taste (I use 3 tbsp.)
2 to 3 cups shrimp, cooked & cleaned
2 cans condensed shrimp soup (2 ½ c.)
¼ cup sliced almonds toasted
paprika to garnish

DIRECTIONS:

Preheat oven to 350 degrees. Saute celery & pepper in butter until soft. Add to other ingredients. Pour into 2 qt. baking dish. Garnish with paprika. Bake for 25-30 minutes or until bubbly.

Evelyn McCain

CRABMEAT AU GRATIN

8 tbsp. butter
1 lb. crabmeat (I like to use claw meat or lump)
1 rib of celery
2 onions
2 green onions
2 tbsp. parsley
1 can cream of onion or cream of mushroom soup
1 cup grated Velveeta cheese

Sauté onion, green onion and celery until soft. Add crabmeat, soup and cheese. When blended, add parsley. Bake at 350 degrees until heated through and bubbly.

Serve over Pepperidge Farms bake & serve pastry puffs

Mary Ann Campbell

FISH & SHRIMP DELIGHT

1 lb. package of frozen fish filets
(sole, cod, haddock or halibut)

2 tbsp. butter or margarine

black pepper to taste

1 can cream of shrimp soup
(can use frozen shrimp soup thawed)

¼ cup shredded Parmesan cheese

lemon or lime wedges

paprika for garnish

Thaw fish enough to separate. Place in buttered baking dish. Sprinkle with black pepper and dot with 2 tablespoons of butter or margarine. Add can of cream of shrimp soup. Top with shredded cheese and sprinkle paprika over cheese.

Bake at 400 degrees for 25 minutes. Serve with lemon or lime wedges. Serves 4

Mrs. Joe Bellenfant

HERBED SHRIMP & FETA CASSEROLE

2 large eggs
1 c. evaporated milk
4 cloves garlic, minced
1 c. plain yogurt
1 lb. med. peeled shrimp, uncooked
½ lb. shredded Mozzarella cheese
1 lb. medium shrimp, peeled
8 oz. Feta cheese, shredded
½ lb. shredded Mozzarella cheese
½ lb. cooked angel hair pasta
1- 16 oz. jar mild chunky salsa
1-5 oz. pkg. Swiss cheese
1 tsp. basil
1 tsp. oregano
1 c. chopped parsley
1 tsp. Worcestershire sauce

Preheat oven to 350 degrees. Coat bottom and sides of an 8 x 12 inch baking dish with cooking spray. In separate bowl, blend eggs, milk, yogurt, Feta and Swiss cheese, parsley, basil, oregano and garlic. Spread half of cooked pasta over bottom of baking dish. Cover with salsa, add half of shrimp and spread remaining pasta over shrimp. Pour and spread egg mixture over pasta. Add remaining shrimp and top with Mozzarella cheese. Bake at 350 degrees for 30 minutes. Remove from oven and let stand for 10 minutes before serving.

Michelle Baldwin

MOTHER'S OYSTER CASSEROLE

1 large container of fresh shucked oysters, drained - or 2 cans
2 tubes (1/2 of box) of saltine crackers, crushed
1 tbsp. Worcestershire sauce
1 tsp. black pepper
½ stick butter, melted
2 cups milk
½ stick butter in pats

Mix all ingredients together except milk and cold butter. Place in 2 quart baking dish that has been buttered or sprayed with cooking spray. Pour milk over mixture. Add ½ stick butter to top in pats. Bake at 325 degrees for 35 to 40 minutes or until bubbly.

Genice Johnson

SEAFOOD CASSEROLE

1 cup herbed bread crumbs
1 lb. fish cut into 1 inch pieces
¼ lb. crabmeat
¼ lb. scallops, cut into small pieces
¼ lb. small shrimp
1 can cheddar cheese soup (10 oz.)
Cooked rice

DIRECTIONS:
Put all ingredients in casserole dish and cover with cheddar cheese soup. I make this the night before. Then all I do is boil the rice while I'm cooking the casserole.

Bake at 400 degrees for 30 minutes.

Catherine Brent

SHRIMP CHEESE CASSEROLE

2 cups boiled rice
2/3 lb. grated Velveeta cheese
2 eggs, beaten well
½ cup salad oil
2/3 tsp. salt
1 onion, minced
1- 14 ½ oz. can evaporated milk
2 cups cooked shrimp

Mix well. Bake in greased casserole dish.

Bake at 350 degrees for 1 hour.

Sally Burch

SHRIMP MOUSSE

2 envelopes unflavored gelatin
½ c. cold water
1 can (10 oz.) tomato soup, undiluted
1 pkg. cream cheese (8 oz.)
1 c. mayonnaise
2 tbsp. lemon juice
2 tbsp. Worcestershire sauce
1-2 tbsp. hot sauce (I use 2)
1/4 c. finely chopped onion
½ c. finely chopped bell pepper
½ c. finely chopped celery
1 -2 ¼ to 4 ¼ oz. can ripe
black olives, chopped
1 tsp. dried crushed parsley
2 pkg. fresh frozen salad shrimp (6 oz. pkg.) or
2 (4 ½ oz.) cans small shrimp, drained

Soften gelatin in cold water. Set aside. Heat soup in large heavy sauce pan; add cream cheese. Cook over medium heat, stirring constantly until mixture is smooth.

Stir in softened gelatin, mayonnaise, lemon juice, Worcestershire sauce and hot sauce. Add remaining ingredients, mixing well.

Spoon into a 7- cup mold and chill until firm. Remove from mold and garnish as desired.

"MAMIE"

SHRIMP PASTA SALAD

3 tbsp. cold water
2 tbsp. milk
2 tbsp. chili sauce
1 tsp. horseradish
1 pkg. Suddenly Salad Italian pasta and salad mix
1/3 cup mayonnaise or salad dressing
2 tbsp. chili sauce
Parmesan cheese
1 medium tomato, seeded, chopped
(or use grape tomatoes, halved)
1 stalk celery chopped (or buy the equivalent chopped from the salad bar)
12 to 15 large fully cooked shrimp (I buy frozen shrimp that have already been cooked)

Prepare pasta and vegetables as directed on package. Stir seasoning mix, mayonnaise, water, milk, chili sauce, horseradish and Parmesan cheese in bowl until blended. Stir in pasta, vegetables, tomato and celery. Gently fold in shrimp. Can serve at this point or refrigerate. 4-6 servings.

Pat Iannacone

MEAT & POULTRY

Notes...

BEEF FILLETS WITH PORTOBELLO SAUCE

6 (6 oz.) beef tenderloin fillets
½ tsp. freshly ground pepper
5 tbsp. butter, divided
1/3 c. dry red wine
½ c. sour cream
2 tsp. chopped fresh tarragon
1 tbsp. kosher salt
8 oz. Portobello mushroom caps, sliced
3 oz. Stilton or bleu cheese, crumbled & divided

GARNISH: Fresh tarragon sprigs

Rub fillets with tarragon, salt & pepper. Melt 2 tbsp. butter in a large skillet over medium-high heat. Cook fillets 4-5 minutes on each side or to desired degrees of doneness. Remove from skillet and keep warm.

Melt remaining 3 tbsp. butter in skillet. Add mushrooms, sauté 3-4 minutes or until tender. Add wine and cook 1-2 minutes, stirring to loosen particles from bottom of skillet. Stir in sour cream. Sprinkle ¼ c. cheese into sauce, stirring until melted.

Arrange fillets on a serving platter and drizzle with sauce. Sprinkle with remaining cheese and garnish.

Pegine Hill

BEEF ROAST

3 lb. sirloin tip beef roast
1 can cream of mushroom soup
pepper (onion soup provides salt)
1 pkg. Lipton onion soup
dash of 91 Sauce

Line a heavy large container with heavy-duty foil. Place 2 large pieces of foil each way of container. Place roast inside. Add other ingredients. Wrap the foil to cover and bake at 400 degrees for 30 minutes. Turn oven down to 350 degrees and cook 2-3 hours. Makes good gravy – easy to fix. Serves 6 – 8.

Jean Glass

BOURBON-GLAZED PORK CHOPS

½ c. firmly packed light brown sugar
2 tbsp. bourbon
6 bone-in pork chops (1 inch thick)
3 tbsp. Dijon mustard
2 tbsp. soy sauce
½ tsp. salt
¼ tsp. pepper

Set pork chops aside. Mix all other ingredients in a shallow dish or large zip lock plastic bag. Add pork chops, cover or seal, and chill 30 minutes, turning once. Remove pork from marinade – reserving marinade.

Grill pork, covered with grill lid, over medium-high heat (350-400 degrees) about 10-12 minutes or until meat thermometer registers 160 degrees, turning once.

Bring reserved marinade to a boil in a small saucepan, stirring occasionally, 2 minutes. Pour over chops. Good with rice!

Lynne Hutson

LEMON-OLIVE MEAT BALLS

1 lb. lean ground beef or turkey
4 oz. grated sharp cheese
½ c. milk
1 c. soft bread crumbs
12 slices bacon, partially cooked
3 tbsp. lemon juice
1 tsp. salt
12 green stuffed olives & ¼ green pepper, finely chopped
1 egg, beaten

Mix all ingredients lightly together, except the bacon. Gently shape into 12 balls. Wrap a bacon strip around each ball and fasten with a toothpick.

Bake at 350 degrees for 40 minutes.

LaVelle Leopard

MEAT LOAF

1 ½ lbs. ground beef
1 c. fresh oats
small pieces green pepper, chopped
½ c. tomato sauce
1 egg
1 small onion, chopped
1 ½ tsp. salt
¼ tsp. black pepper

Mix all ingredients well.

SAUCE:
½ can tomatoes
2 tbsp. vinegar
1 c. water
2 tbsp. mustard
2 tbsp. brown sugar

Mix well, pour over meat loaf, and bake for 1 ½ hours at 350 degrees or until done.

Lois Pratt

TENDERLOIN OF BEEF WELLINGTON

3 lb. beef tenderloin
1 tsp. salt
1 egg
brown sauce
2 sheets puff pastry
2 tbsp. soft butter
½ tsp. pepper
1 tbsp. water
mushroom filling

Pre-heat oven to 425 degrees. Tie roast in several points of meat. Place on rack in shallow pan. Spread top with butter (sides also). Sprinkle with salt and pepper. Bake 20 minutes. Remove from oven, and cool – about 30 minutes. Remove string and pat dry.

(continued on next page)

Make mushroom filling. In a medium skillet, combine 1 lb. fresh mushrooms (finely chopped), ½ c. chopped onion, ½ c. dry sherry, ¼ c. butter and ¼ c. snipped parsley. Stir well and cook until onion is tender and liquid absorbed.

On a well-floured surface, roll out pastry into rectangle about 14x16 cut to make even. Heat oven to 400 degrees. Place tenderloin at edge of long side of pastry. Spread mushroom filling on remaining surface of pastry, leaving 1 inch margin on each side. Roll tenderloin and pastry. Seal seam and ends securely, moistening with water as needed. Carefully place pastry-wrapped meat seam side down on baking sheet. Roll out leftover pastry – cut leaves, flowers or stars to garnish. Mix egg and water and brush over top and all sides of pastry.

Bake for 30 minutes or until pastry is golden brown. Serve with brown sauce as follows:

BROWN SAUCE FOR BEEF WELLINGTON

In sauce pan combine the following:

2 c. beef bouillon	½ cup dry sherry
3 tbsp. finely chopped onion	3 tbsp. finely chopped carrot
1 tbsp. finely chopped celery	2 sprigs parsley
1 bay leaf, crumbled	1/8 tsp. crushed thyme leaves

Simmer for 30 minutes. Strain mixture through sieve. Discard vegetable mixture. Stir in 3 tbsp. dry sherry. Simmer 5 minutes longer. Stir in 2 tbsp. butter, a little at a time.

I cook the meat (its first 30 minutes) and make mushroom filling and brown sauce the day before.

Beverly Isdell

BAKED CHICKEN CORDON BLEU

6 chicken breast halves
1 ½ c. Italian bread crumbs
6 thin slices cheese (Swiss, Mozzarella) from a block
6 thin slices ham
6 butter slices (1 tbsp.)
1 egg

Place chicken between sheet of plastic wrap or waxed paper. Lightly pound chicken with a meat mallet until ¼ inch thick. Lay chicken breast out. Place ham slice, butter and cheese slice inside.

Roll chicken up from ends, dip in egg and then bread crumbs. Place chicken, seam down, in greased pan. Cook at 425 degrees for 35 minutes.

Christy Wampler

CHEESY CHICKEN

1 stick butter
1 can mushroom soup
Pepperidge Farm corn bread stuffing
1 pkg. skinless, boneless chicken
4-5 slices American cheese
dry red cooking wine

Grease corningware pan with butter. Put in chicken after removing fat. Place American cheese slices on top. Mix ½ stick melted butter, soup, and 3 tablespoons to ¼ cup wine together.

Spread on top of cheese. Place stuffing crumbs on top – enough to cover. Pour remaining butter on top. Cook at 350 degrees about 45 minutes. Serves 4.

Elaine Wilson

CHICKEN ARTICHOKE

4 skinless chicken breasts
1 can cream of chicken soup (10 ¾ oz., 98% fat free)
1 can artichokes, not marinated
salt and pepper
1 tbsp. butter
½ soup can white wine
1 can sliced mushrooms
1 tbsp. capers, minced and drained

Brown chicken breasts in butter. Mix wine and soup and pour over chicken breasts which have been placed in a 9x13 inch glass pyrex dish. Add artichokes, capers, and salt and pepper. Bake at 350 degrees for 50 minutes. Serve over rice. Yields 4 servings.

Margaret Reeves

CHICKEN ENCHILADAS

8 oz. carton sour cream
½ c. chopped onion
1 can cream of chicken soup
4-5 chicken breasts, cooked and diced
2 ½ c. shredded cheddar cheese
1 tsp. cumin
dash hot pepper
1 small can green chilies
10-12 flour tortillas
1 small can Carnation milk

Place chicken on tortillas and roll up. Put toothpick on top to hold tortilla together. Mix all other ingredients together and pour over top of tortillas. Add cheese and bake at 350 degrees for 20-25 minutes.

Pam Greer

CHICKEN POT PIE

Pastry for 2 crust pie
6 tbsp. butter
¼ tsp. pepper
2/3 c. half and half
1 ½ c. mixed vegetables
(I use potatoes, corn, carrots, frozen green peas, green onions, broccoli.)
6 tbsp. flour
½ tsp. salt
2 c. chicken broth
2 c. cooked chopped chicken

In a saucepan melt butter, add flour, salt and pepper. Stir until mixed and heated completely. Slowly add chicken broth and half and half, stirring until thickened. Add vegetables and chicken. Pour into pastry lined pan. (I use a 9x13 inch casserole pan). Cut second pastry into strips and place in lattice design on top of dish. Bake at 425 degrees for 35-40 minutes. Serves 6 – 8.

Debbie Connell

CHICKEN-RICE ROGER

2 ½ lb. cut-up fryer
  or 2 pkg. chicken breasts
½ stick margarine
1 tbsp. grated onion or ½ clove minced garlic
2 chicken bouillon cubes dissolved in 1¾ c. water or
  2 tsp. instant chicken bouillon.
¾ c. uncooked rice
3 oz. can sliced mushrooms
salt & pepper to taste

Flour and brown chicken in a little oil. While it is browning, put rice, salt and pepper in greased casserole dish and sprinkle grated onion on top. Add mushrooms (juice and all). Arrange chicken on top. Pour bouillon over it all. Dot with butter. Bake for 1 hour at 350 degrees.

Peggy Randolph

CHICKEN ROTEL

2-4 c. chopped cooked chicken
1 small onion, chopped
1 lb. Velvetta cheese, cut in small pieces
1 can Rotel tomatoes, undrained & chopped
7 oz. pkg. Angel-hair spaghetti
1 small can green peas, drained
1 small green pepper, chopped

Saute onion and pepper in butter. Cook and drain spaghetti. Mix all ingredients together. Put in large lightly-buttered casserole dish. Bake at 350 degrees for 30 minutes.

Jane DeFord

CREAMED CHICKEN OVER CORNBREAD

1/4 c. butter, margarine, or chicken fat
2 c. cooked chicken, diced
¼ c. pimentos
1 c. milk
1/3 c. all purpose flour
½ tsp. salt
1 can sliced mushrooms (3 oz.) drained (optional)
1 c. chicken broth

In sauce pan melt butter, margarine, or chicken fat. Blend in flour and salt. Add chicken broth and milk all at once.

Cool. Stirring constantly, until sauce is thick and bubbly.

Add chicken, mushrooms and pimentos. Heat thoroughly and serve over cornbread. Makes 5 servings.

Charles Wilson

EASY CHICKEN POT PIE

3 chicken breasts, cooked & cubed
1 box Pillsbury roll out crusts
1 egg
1 can cream of chicken soup
2 cans veg-all vegetables
butter

Cook chicken in microwave with ¼ cup of water. Sprinkle with chicken bouillon sprinkles and curry powder for more taste. Don't overcook. Drain and cube.

Mix soup and drained veg-alls. Combine with chicken mixture. Pour mixture into pie crust in a large pie plate. Dot with butter. Cut a design in second pie crust and place on top. Beat one egg and brush pie.

Cook at 350 – 375 degrees for about 45 minutes. Cool 15 minutes before serving.

Carol Schmidt

FRIED CHICKEN

chicken parts
flour to coat chicken
2 eggs
salt & pepper

Beat eggs in a bowl. Dip chicken in eggs then flour, salt and pepper parts. Place chicken in electric skillet with 2 cups oil at 350 degrees. Turn every 15 minutes until done or golden brown. Place on paper towels to remove oil.

Wilma Hood

MAMA'S CHICKEN AND DUMPLINGS

Chicken broth from a cooked chicken with some small pieces of chicken.

Dumplings:
- 2 c. flour
- dash salt
- 1 ½ tsp. baking powder
- ¼ c. shortening

Mix together dry ingredients and then cut in shortening. Add ice water until biscuit dough consistency. Roll out thin and cut into 2 inch squares. Heat broth until boiling and add 1 chicken bouillon cube. Salt and pepper to taste. Drop dumplings into boiling broth and cover and cook for 15 minutes.

Sandra Shoemake

MEXICAN CHICKEN

1 chicken
1 can cream of chicken soup
1 can cream of mushroom soup
1 tbsp. chili powder
Doritos
1 tbsp. garlic powder
½ green pepper, chopped
1 ½ c. grated cheese
1 can Ro-Tel tomatoes

Boil chicken in salt water until tender. De-bone and chop. Mix together all ingredients except cheese and Doritos.

In a buttered dish layer Doritos – chicken mixture – cheese. Do this twice. Leave off top layer of cheese. Bake at 350 degrees for 1½ hours. Remove and cover with cheese. Return to oven until cheese melts.

Louise Westbrook

WHITE BAR-B-QUE SAUCE FOR CHICKEN

1 ½ c. mayonnaise
¼ c. sugar
¼ c. Worcestershire sauce
pepper to taste
½ c. lemon juice
¼ c. vinegar
4 tsp. salt

Mix all ingredients. Allow flavors to blend at room temperature for 15 minutes before use. Brush on chicken pieces several times during last 15 minutes of cooking. Makes enough for 1 chicken. Store any leftover sauce in refrigerator.

Julie Adams

MOM'S RECIPES

Notes...

Mom's Memo

My wish for you, my daughter, is to love God, be happy, honest and a friend to man. You have been a kind and loving daughter. I cannot mention you without mentioning my son-in-law, Brent, who has the same qualities. I am proud of you both. God bless you.

Mom Wilson

Here are a few of my favorite recipes.....

CARAMEL ICING
(With caramelized sugar)

3 c. sugar
1 slightly beaten egg
½ tsp. pure vanilla extract
¾ c. canned milk
1 stick butter
4 marshmallows

Melt ½ c. sugar in iron skillet on low heat to caramelize. Mix butter, eggs, remaining sugar and milk. Turn stove on medium heat. When it begins to boil, add caramelized sugar. Cook until soft ball stage when dropped into a cup of water (about 5 minutes). Remove from heat. Add marshmallows and vanilla extract. Let cool slightly. Beat until right consistency to spread.

(I pour my icing over the cake and pull on toward sides with knife until cool.)

KLEEMAN'S APPLE PIE

1 tbsp. flour
½ tsp. cinnamon
1 c. sugar
1 sheet pie crust for pastry strips
4 tbsp. butter, melted
¾ c. orange juice
3 medium size, very tart, apples, grated (Granny Smith)

Make pastry or use 1 deep dish unbaked pie crust. Sift flour and cinnamon into melted butter. Add orange juice and sugar. Mix together. Place chopped apples into pastry shell and pour above ingredients over them.

Put strips of pastry over top forming lattice work. (Sprinkle with sugar). Bake 15 minutes in 450 degree oven. Reduce heat to 300 degrees and bake until done (about 25 minutes longer).

PIE CRUST: (Will make 4-5 shells)

3 c. plain flour
1 tsp. salt
1 c. Crisco plus 2 tbsp.
5 tbsp. water
1 tbsp. vinegar
1 egg, beaten

With pastry blender, blend flour and salt with shortening. Mix beaten egg with water and vinegar. Add flour to mixture, blend well. Let dough rest 5 minutes. Roll to fit pan.

SCALLOPED OYSTERS

4 pts. fresh oysters (small stewing oysters)
1 ½ sticks butter
5 c. Keebler crackers, crushed
1 ½ c. Half and Half, cream or milk

Sprinkle with McCormick Hot-Shot seasoned pepper.

Melt butter and add cracker crumbs. Wash oysters and fill a baking dish with alternate layers of oysters and buttered cracker crumbs. Sprinkle each layer of oysters with pepper and add ½ of cream.

Do not put more than two layers. Moisten top layer of crackers with remaining cream. Bake at 350 degrees for 30 minutes or until oysters are done.

STRAWBERRY PRESERVES

3 pts. sugar
3 pts. strawberries

Wash and cap strawberries and slice. In a large vessel on medium heat, start with:

(1) 1 pint sugar and 1 pint berries. Cook 5 minutes, stirring while you cook.
(2) Same as #1.
(3) Same as #1 except cook for 10 minutes.

Skim foam during last 5 minutes. Let preserves get cold, stirring at intervals to plump. Put in sterilized jars and use paraffin to seal.

PASTA

Notes...

CHRISTY'S PASTA

1 box bowtie pasta (1 lb.)
1 can white chicken breast meat (small or large)
salt
1 can cream of chicken soup
milk
butter
pepper

Boil bowtie pasta until tender and drain. Add chicken and soup. Mix well. Add butter, milk, salt and pepper to desired taste and consistency. Heat on low until warm enough to serve. Great with peas and carrots!

Christy Irwin

EASY LASAGNA

1 lb. hamburger
2 ½ cans tomatoes (3 ½ c.)
1 envelope spaghetti sauce mix
1 -8 oz. pkg. Parmesan cheese (use ½ pkg.)
1 can tomato sauce (8 oz.)
1 c. cream cottage cheese
8 oz. Mozzarella cheese
1 pkg. lasagna noodles (8 oz.) (I use ¾ pkg.)

Brown meat slowly and drain off excess fat. Add tomatoes, tomato sauce, and spaghetti sauce mix. Cover and simmer 40-60 minutes. Salt to taste.

Cook noodles. Place ½ of the noodles in an 11 ½ x 7 ½ inch pan. Then cover with ½ sauce, ½ Mozzarella cheese and ½ cottage cheese. Repeat layers, ending with sauce on top. Then top with Parmesan cheese.

Bake at 350 degrees for 30-35 minutes.

Belinda Tidwell

FETTUCINE ALFREDO

1 lb. fettucine
1 c. Parmesan cheese, grated
1 egg yolk
1 c. unsalted butter
½ c. heavy cream
black pepper

Cook fettucine 8-10 minutes. Mix egg yolk together with cream, set aside. Heat butter in sauce pan until melted. Add to noodles and toss off heat. Add cheese and toss on low heat until partially melted. Add cream and toss off heat. Pepper to taste.

For added creaminess and saucier noodles, add 1 to 2 extra egg yolks to cream.

Heidi and Carl Wallace

GREEK MEAT SAUCE

3 shallots, finely diced, browned in olive oil
4 small cans tomato sauce
1 tsp. ground cinnamon
freshly ground pepper to taste
1 stick cinnamon*
½ c. dry red wine
2 -3 lbs. ground round
2 tbsp. minced garlic
1 large can diced tomatoes
1 tsp. ground nutmeg
1 ½ tsp. salt
1 ½ tsp. whole mixed pickling spice*

*(tie these in cheesecloth bag).

Brown ground round in large dutch oven. Add browned shallots and all other ingredients. Stir to mix well. Cover and simmer gently, stirring occasionally for 3-4 hours. Let sauce cool and skim any fat. Serve over pasta of your choice (I prefer angel hair), or refrigerate or freeze. Best prepared one day ahead to let flavors "marry".

Pegine Hill

HOLIDAY TURKETTI

5 ½ c. diced cooked chicken or turkey
8 oz. pkg. elbow spaghetti
1 small can chopped pimento
¾ lb. American cheese, grated
2 cans cream of celery soup
1 c. chicken broth
1 green pepper, chopped
1 small onion, chopped

Mix broth with soup. Put chicken, onion, green pepper and pimento in big roaster and pour soup mixture over. Put in cheese. Cook spaghetti, drain and pour into mixture while hot. Mix well. Salt and pepper to taste.

Put in 2 greased pyrex dishes. Bake at 350 degrees for 30 minutes. Freezes well. If frozen, take it out and let thaw and bake 10 or 15 minutes more.

Jean Fleming

MAMA'S SPAGHETTI

2 ½ lbs. ground beef
2 large green bell peppers, chopped
¼ c. Worcestershire sauce
salt, pepper & sugar to taste
1 c. chopped onion
2 sticks real butter
1 pint tomato puree
1 large can tomato soup

Boil 1½ lbs. of spaghetti and drain. Brown beef, onions, and peppers. Drain grease and add other ingredients. Simmer sauce for 45 minutes. Add spaghetti. Serves 12.

This is my mother's famous spaghetti recipe that we still enjoy.

Linda Carden

MAMA'S SPAGHETTI DISH

1 pkg. Angel Hair pasta (10 oz.)
1 lb. hamburger or ground turkey
1 large can tomato sauce
1 medium onion, chopped
1 c. sharp cheddar cheese, grated
½ tsp. salt
½ tsp. pepper
½ c. milk
dash chili powder

Cook spaghetti. Mix onion, hamburger, salt, pepper and chili powder and simmer until meat is done. Drain. Mix tomato sauce and milk in another bowl. Put layer of spaghetti in baking dish. Layer meat, then sauce and milk mixture. Top with cheese. Bake at 350 degrees for 30 minutes. (Does well in crockpot.)

Sandra Selle

MAZZETTI

1 lb. ground beef
1 can tomato soup
1 can cream of mushroom soup
shredded cheddar cheese
1 onion
1 small can mushrooms
8 oz. pkg. noodles

Brown onion and ground beef. Drain and add tomato soup and cream of mushroom soup. Season with salt, pepper, garlic powder, chili powder and Italian seasoning.

Cook noodles and mix with above. Put in baking dish and top with cheddar cheese. Bake at 350 degrees until cheese melts.

FAMILY OF WALTER J. "JOEY" DAVIS

MOM'S BEST MEATBALLS
(Doug's favorite)

1 lb. ground round
1 lb. ground pork
1 lb. ground veal
1 egg
¼ c. plain bread crumbs
2/3 c. grated parmesan cheese
1 grated onion
¼ c. chopped fresh parsley
1 clove garlic
seasalt to taste
3 tbsp. ketchup

Mix all ingredients together and make into balls. Cook in 350 degree oven on broiler pan for about 30 minutes. Transfer to your favorite marinara sauce on stove and simmer. Serve with pasta and salad. Fabulous!!

Brenda Franks Hale

PASTA A LA CAPRESE

12 plum or 4 large tomatoes, sliced thin lengthwise
3-4 cloves smashed garlic
20 leaves fresh basil, torn in half
freshly ground black pepper
8 oz. grated Mozzarella cheese
1 long thin yellow-red sweet pepper, sliced thin
¼ c. good quality fruity olive oil
salt & garlic salt to taste

Serve with freshly grated romano (Locatelli is an excellent cheese).

At least 1 ½ hours before serving, combine tomatoes, garlic, sweet pepper, basil, oil, salt and pepper in a large bowl. Cover and let stand without refrigeration. When pasta is cooked and well drained, add 1/2 sauce, then Mozzarella. Mix quickly and add rest of sauce. Serve immediately. Pass pecorino romano.

Pasta: 1 lb. Penneziti or Rigatoni.

Marty Cognata

"SKETTI-SKILLET"

½ lb. hamburger
1 can tomato sauce
2 c. water
6 oz. broken spaghetti
salt & pepper to taste
½ c. onions and peppers, chopped
½ lb. bulk sausage
1 can diced tomatoes
2 celery ribs, chopped
½ tsp. Italian seasoning

In a large skillet brown meat, onions, peppers and celery. Add remaining ingredients. Bring to boil. Reduce heat, cover and simmer 15 minutes. Quick & easy on busy night! Serves 4-6. Yummy!

Dawn Duclos

SALADS & DRESSINGS

Notes...

BLUE CHEESE VINAIGRETTE

4 oz. blue cheese (crumbled)
2 garlic cloves (mashed whole)
salt and pepper
1 tbsp. white vinegar
vegetable oil

Combine the blue cheese, salt, pepper, garlic and vinegar in a mason jar. Pour oil over mixture. You want approximately 1 to 1 ½ cups of oil and you want the dressing to be a little thick, so just enough oil to cover the dressing. Mix well with spoon and shake.

Melissa Davis

CORNBREAD SALAD

1 pkg. Mexican cornbread mix (6 oz.)
1 c. mayonnaise
1 c. chopped green pepper
8 oz. shredded cheddar cheese
2 cans pinto beans (16 oz.), drained
10 slices crumbled bacon
1 carton (8 oz.) sour cream
1 pkg. ranch style (1 oz.) salad dressing mix
3 large tomatoes
1 bunch chopped green onions
2 cans whole kernel corn, drained (16 oz.)

Prepare cornbread according to package directions. Cool. Crumble half of cornbread into bowl. Top with half of other ingredients. Repeat layers. Cover and chill for 2 hours. Yields 8-10 servings. Enjoy!

Barbara Noland

CRANBERRY CHICKEN SALAD

Dissolve 1 envelope Knox gelatin in ¼ c. water. Add:

1 can whole cranberry sauce
½ c. chopped pecans
1 (9 oz.) can crushed pineapple, with liquid
1 tbsp. lemon juice

Let set in large mold 8 hours.

Second layer:
Dissolve 1 envelope Knox gelatin in 1 c. water. Do not boil. Add:

1 c. mayonnaise
3 tbsp. lemon juice
2 c. diced chicken
2 tbsp. fresh chopped parsley
½ c. chicken broth
¾ tsp. salt
½ c. diced celery

Pour over first layer. Chill. Serve on lettuce. Serves 8.

Charles & Carol Bond

CRANBERRY SALAD

2 oranges
2 ½ c. fresh cranberries
3 pkg. orange jello (3 oz.)
3 c. boiling water
2 tbsp. lemon juice
1 c. sugar
pinch of salt
1 ½ c. chopped celery
1 c. pineapple, undrained
½ c. chopped pecans

Peel oranges. Put peeling and cranberries thru food grinder. Section oranges. Dissolve jello in boiling water; add lemon juice, sugar, and salt. Stir until sugar is dissolved. Add orange sections, cranberry mixture, celery, pineapple, and pecans. Mix well. Pour into 10 cup mold and chill until set. Serves 12-15.

NOTE: Salad is best if made at least 2 days before serving.

Carolyn Dodson

CRUNCHY CHICKEN SALAD

1 c. mayonnaise
¾ c. sour cream
2 c. diced celery
1 c. halved cashews
1 ½ tbsp. lemon juice
2 ½ tsp. salt
5 c. diced cooked chicken

Combine mayonnaise, sour cream, juice and salt. Add celery, cashews and chicken. Toss lightly and serve on lettuce. Serves 8-10.

Charles & Carol Bond

"ENGLISH PEA SALAD"

1 can English peas (16 oz.) (drained)
1 can shoe peg corn (drained)
4-oz. jar drained pimento
1 can French green beans (drained)
1 c. diced onion
1 c. chopped green pepper
1 c. chopped celery

DRESSING:

¾ c. cider vinegar
½ c. oil
½ tsp. salt
1 c. sugar
1 tsp. black pepper

Stir unti dissolved. Pour over salad. Make one day ahead.

Joyce P. Liggett

FOUR BEAN SALAD

1 can cut yellow wax
beans (15 oz.)
1 can dark red kidney
beans (15 oz.)
2/3 c. sugar
½ c. apple cider vinegar
1 tsp. celery seeds
3 cloves minced garlic
or ¾ tsp. garlic powder
1 can black beans (15 oz.)
1/3 c. chopped yellow onion
1 can Progresso
cannellini beans (20 oz.)
½ c. vegetable oil
(some of the vinegar
may be balsamic)
½ tsp. each of celery salt
and kosher salt

Drain and rinse beans. Combine remaining ingredients in large bowl. Stir to dissolve sugar. Add beans to mixture. Refrigerate 12 hours before serving. This keeps refrigerated for 2 weeks. It's colorful. Great for picnics!

Marilyn Lehew

FROZEN CHERRY SALAD

1 pkg. cream cheese (8 oz.)
softened
1 can cherry pie filling (21 oz.)
1 carton (8 oz). frozen
whipped topping, thawed
2 cans mandarin oranges.
(11 oz.) drained

In a mixing bowl, combine cream cheese and whipped topping. Stir in pie filling. Set aside ¼ c. oranges for garnish. Fold remaining oranges into cream cheese mixture. Transfer to a 9 x 5 x 5 inch loaf pan. Cover and freeze overnight. Remove from the freezer 15 minutes before cutting.

Lucille Isaacs

FROZEN CRANBERRY SALAD

2 (3 oz.) pkg. softened cream cheese
1 can whole cranberry sauce
1 small can crushed pineapple
1 c. whipped cream
2 tbsp. mayonnaise
1 c. chopped pecans
2 tbsp. sugar
miniature marshmallows, if desired

Combine all ingredients and fold in 1 cup whipped cream. Freeze.

"MAMIE"

FRUIT SALAD

1 can sliced peaches (16 oz.)
1 can sliced pears (16 oz.)
1 can pineapple chunks (16 oz.)
1 can apricot halves (16 oz.)
12 soft coconut macaroons
2 bananas, sliced
1 tsp. lemon juice
¼ c. oleo
1/3 c. Amaretto
3 oz. almonds, sliced or chopped – toasted

Drain fruits and combine. Mix banana slices with lemon juice and add to other fruits. Toss gently. Layer half of the fruit mixture and macaroon crumbs in a 2 ½ qt. baking dish. Sprinkle with half the almonds and oleo. Repeat procedure. Pour Amaretto lightly over the mixture (optional – fruit juice). Bake at 350 degrees for 30 minutes. Serves 12. Great with ham!

Virginia Hill

GINGER ALE SALAD

2 large pkg. lemon jello
2 c. boiling water
1 can chopped pimentos
1 c. chopped celery
2 c. ginger ale
1 tbsp. sugar
1 - #2 can crushed pineapple
2 c. chopped pecans

Dissolve jello in boiling water. Add ginger ale and sugar. After thoroughly mixed, add rest of ingredients and pour into molds and refrigerate. Pretty at Christmas – but good anytime!

Wanda Luna

"GRAPE SALAD"

Wash and drain well

4 c. white grapes
4 c. red grapes

Mix together:
8 oz. sour cream
½ c. sugar
8 oz. cream cheese
1 tsp. vanilla

Fold in grapes.

TOPPING:
1 c. chopped pecans
½ c. light brown sugar
Refrigerate all overnight.

Doris Alexander

ILLINOIS SALAD

baby spinach greens
sliced black olives
Balsamic vinegar
pine nuts
Feta cheese
olive oil

Quantities depend on size of salad desired. Use greens as bulk of salad and add other ingredients, garnishing to taste.

Carol Camp

"KRAUT SALAD"

1 large can shredded kraut, well drained
1 small can pimento, chopped
½-1 chopped whole green pepper
1 tbsp. celery seed
dash of powdered ginger (opt.)
1 c. white granulated sugar
½ c. white vinegar
½ c. chopped green onion, tops and all
1 tbsp. mustard seed
1/8 tsp. paprika (optional)
½ c. salad oil

Bring to a boil the sugar and white vinegar. Set aside to cool. Mix together the shredded kraut, pimento, onion, green pepper, mustard seed and celery seed. Pour the oil over the mixture and toss well. Then pour the sugar and vinegar mixture (be sure it has cooled) over the kraut mixture. Toss well. Marinate for at least 24 hours in the refrigerator. Stir at least twice during the 24 hours that the salad is marinating. This salad will keep for days refrigerated.

.

Katie K. White

LIME SALAD

1 box lime jello
1 small can crushed pineapple
1 c. chopped celery
1 small pkg. cream cheese
1 c. chopped nuts
1 c. grated carrots

Dissolve jello in 1 cup of boiling water. Drain juice from pineapple. Add cream cheese with juice then combine all ingredients and congeal.

Catherine L. Grice

MANDARIN ALMOND SALAD

1 bag Boston or butter lettuce
1 pt. raspberries (optional)
2 tbsp. sugar
1 – 2 oz. bag slivered almonds
1 kiwi, sliced (optional)
4 green onions, sliced
1 – 10 oz. can mandarin oranges, drained

Toss lettuce and onions in serving bowl. Arrange oranges, kiwi and raspberries decoratively on top. Heat almonds and sugar in skillet until sugar melts and turns golden brown. Watch carefully. Turn onto waxed paper and cool. Break apart. Put on top of salad.

DRESSING:
¼ c. mango juice or ¼ c. pureed mango pieces
2-3 tbsp. sugar
juice from ½ lime
1 tbsp. seasoned rice vinegar
1-2 tbsp. canola oil
5 drops Tabasco
¼ - ½ tsp. crushed pepper flakes

Mix together early to let flavors blend. Pour over salad before serving.

DeLacy Bellenfant- Layhew

MARINATED GREEN BEAN SALAD

1 can French style green beans, drained
1 medium onion, chopped
1 bell pepper, chopped
1 can small green peas, drained
1 rib celery, chopped
1 jar chopped pimento, drained (2 oz.)

DRESSING – Whip together the following:
1 c. vinegar
½ c. Wesson oil
1 tsp. salt
¾ c. sugar
¼ c. water

.

Combine vegetables, pour on dressing and chill overnight. Drain well before serving.

June Fisher

MEDITERRANEAN SPRING SALAD

½ box fettuccine noodles
2 tbsp. lemon juice
2 tsp. oregano
tomato wedges
cucumbers
½ c. olive oil
1 clove garlic
¼ tsp. salt
onion
½ c. Feta cheese

Cook noodles. Drain and cool slightly. Place in shallow bowl. Combine oil, lemon juice, garlic, oregano and salt. Mix well. Pour over noodles and marinate. Combine with other ingredients and serve.

Amy Sanders

METHODIST SLAW

2 small bags chopped cabbage or
 1 head cabbage (3 lb.)
1 tsp. celery seed
1 medium onion, chopped
1 red or green bell pepper
 (or some of each) chopped

May use 1 small can pimentos for color if no red pepper. Blend with cabbage mixture in large container.

DRESSING:
1 c. vinegar
1 c. Wesson oil
1 tbsp. salt
1 c. sugar
1 tsp. powdered mustard
 or ½ tsp. prepared mustard

Pour hot dressing over cabbage mixture. Let stand until blended well. May stir to blend. After cooled, can be refrigerated in containers. The longer it sets – the tastier it is! (I adjust the entire recipe to suit myself.) If too greasy, use less oil or more sugar.

Sue Locke

MIXED GREEN SALAD/SWEET & SOUR DRESSING

1 lb. mixed spring greens
1 bunch green onions or
 red onion rings
½ c. coarsely chopped walnuts
½ c. shredded Parmesan cheese
2 tsp. melted butter
2 oranges, peeled, seeded
 and sectioned
½ c. Feta cheese, crumbled
¼ c. Blue cheese

Mix all above and toss with sweet & sour dressing below:
1 tsp. paprika
1 tsp. dry mustard
½ c. sugar
½ c. vinegar
1 tsp. celery seeds
1 tsp. grated onion
½ c. vegetable oil
1 tsp. salt

For variations to salad, you may use chopped apples, grapes, and pine nuts in place of oranges and walnuts.

Carolyn White

MRS. SHOEMAKE'S FRUIT SALAD

1 large can pineapple with juice
3-4 oranges, in small pieces
maraschino cherries
1 red apple, diced
5 thinly sliced bananas
sugar to taste

Mix all together except bananas. Add bananas just before serving.

Jerry Shoemake

OKRA SALAD

OK, I KNOW WHAT YOU'RE THINKING! But if you like fried okra, you're going to love this unusual salad. The most important point about Okra Salad is that it must be assembled immediately before serving.

The ingredients are simple: prepare equal amounts of fried (breaded) okra, chopped tomatoes and chopped onion. The tomatoes and onions should be room temperature – not cold.

To fry okra, wash and dry the okra pods, then slice about 3/8" thick. Toss the okra pods until the natural stickiness of the okra coats the outside of the pieces. Then toss in corn meal. Fry in vegetable oil at a moderately high temperature until the coating is lightly browned. Drain on paper towels.

Gently toss the fried okra with chopped tomatoes and chopped onion (equal amounts of all three ingredients). Serve immediately.

Nancy James

"PINEAPPLE PRETZEL SALAD"

1 c. crushed pretzels
1 ¼ c. sugar
8 oz. cream cheese, softened
20 oz. can crushed pineapple
1 stick butter, melted
8 oz. container Cool Whip
2 tbsp. cornstarch

Mix together crushed pretzels, melted butter and ½ c. sugar in small bowl until well blended. Press mixture into bottom of 8x8 inch dish to form bottom crust layer. Mix together ½ c. sugar, Cool Whip, and cream cheese in large bowl until mixture is smooth. Spread over first layer.

In a medium saucepan, heat cornstarch, ¼ c. sugar, and juice from drained pineapple. Heat over medium heat until mixture is clear, stirring frequently. Let cool. Add drained pineapple to mixture and spread over second layer.

Let chill for at least 2-3 hours. I freeze it and then let it sit at room temperature for 2 hours before serving. Can be a dessert, too!

Phoebe Fly Smith

PISTACHIO SALAD

1 small box of Jello Pistachio pudding & pie mix
1 can (15 ¼ oz.) crushed pineapple
½ c. nuts
1 can (11 oz.) mandarin oranges
1 c. small marshmallows
9 oz. carton Cool Whip

Pour pudding, fruit and juices together. Then add marshmallows, Cool Whip and nuts. Chill several hours.

Dorothy Garner

SPINACH SALAD

8 slices bacon, cooked and crumbled
Mandarin orange slices
2 lbs. fresh spinach
3 hard boiled eggs

DRESSING:

¾ c. oil (canola or olive)
1/3 c. ketchup
1 small chopped onion
¾ c. sugar
¼ c. red wine vinegar
1 tsp. Worcestershire

Toss salad ingredients. Mix dressing ingredients. Shake well before adding to salad just before serving.

Sandra Selle

SUPER SLAW

1 pkg. slaw mix (16 oz.)
1 pkg. sliced almonds
3 tbsp. sesame seeds
1 pkg. Ramen noodles (chicken flavor)
3 tbsp. red onion, chopped

DRESSING:

¼ c. cider vinegar
½ c. olive oil
½ c. sugar
1 chicken flavor pack from noodles

Remove noodles from package and crumble. Add almonds and sesame seeds. Brown in Teflon skillet in 1 tablespoon butter or oil. Cool.

Heat dressing mixture until sugar dissolves. When cool add red onion. Just before serving, add above mixtures to slaw to preserve crispness.

Mary Ann Crowell

TOSSED STRAWBERRY SALAD

1/2 c. olive or vegetable oil
2-5 tbsp. sugar
¼ c. cider or red wine vinegar
1 garlic clove, minced
¼ tsp. salt
¼ tsp. paprika
pinch white pepper
8 c. torn romaine
4 c. torn bibb lettuce
2 ½ c. sliced fresh strawberries
1 c. (4 oz.) shredded Monterey Jack cheese
½ c. chopped walnuts – toasted

Combine first seven ingredients in jar with tight-fitting lid; shake well.

Just before serving, toss salad greens, strawberries, cheese and walnuts in large salad bowl.

Drizzle with dressing and toss. Yields 6-8 servings.

"Mystery Chef"

SOUPS & STEWS (& CHILI, TOO!)

Notes...

CHEESY POTATO SOUP

2 c. cubed potatoes
1 c. chopped carrots
½ c. chopped celery
½ c. chopped onion
1 can chicken or vegetable broth
salt and pepper to taste
1 ½ c. milk
1 c. shredded cheddar cheese
1 tbsp. parsley, chopped

Combine vegetables and chicken broth and cook until vegetables are tender. Blend in a food processor or mash with a potato masher to the desired consistency. Blend in the milk and cheese. Salt and pepper to taste. Cover and heat until cheese melts. Garnish with parsley.

Leah Karo

CREAM OF SQUASH SOUP

1 large onion, chopped
¼ c. melted butter
3-4 lbs. yellow squash (thinly sliced)
1 ½ tsp. salt
1 tsp. curry powder
extra curry for garnish
3 cloves garlic, minced
2 tbsp. vegetable oil
3-4 c. chicken broth
1 ½ c. Half & Half
½ tsp. white pepper
fresh parsley for garnish, chopped

Saute the onions and garlic in the butter and oil. Stir in squash and chicken broth. Simmer, covered, for 20 minutes or until squash is tender. Stir occasionally. Remove from heat. Spoon 1/3 of mixture into processor. Process until smooth. Repeat twice with remaining squash mixture. Return squash to Dutch Oven. Stir in the Half & Half, salt, white pepper and curry powder. Cook on low heat until heated through. Sprinkle with parsley and extra curry. ENJOY!

Jill Luna

GAZPACHO

4 c. tomato juice
1 medium clove garlic, crushed
1 medium bell pepper, minced
2 scallions, minced
1 tsp. dried tarragon
2 tbsp. red wine vinegar
¼ c. minced fresh parsley
2 c. fresh ripe tomatoes, diced, peeled & seeded
½ c. onion, finely minced
1 tsp. sugar (optional)
1 medium cucumber, peeled, seeded & minced
1 tsp. dried basil
½ tsp. ground cumin
juice of ½ lemon and 1 lime
3 tbsp. extra virgin olive oil
salt, pepper and cayenne to taste

Puree all ingredients in blender. Chill overnight. I always cut up extra tomatoes, cucumber, and scallions to add just before serving. Serve cold. Serves 6. Delicious!

(Taken from "The New Moosewood Cookbook".)

Jan Buck

MEDICINAL CHICKEN SOUP

chicken (2 ½ - 3 lb.)
4 carrots, sliced
6 garlic cloves, pressed
salt and cracked pepper, to taste
½ c. pearl barley
1 large onion, chopped
3-4 ribs celery, coarsely chopped
½ c. fresh parsley or equivalent dried

Cover chicken with water. Boil for 3 hours. Drain chicken – skin and chop. Skim soup and de-fat. Return to pot and add chopped and sliced vegetables. May add a can of chicken broth if you need more liquid. Cook for at least 1 hour longer. Better if made a day ahead.

Cheryl Wilson

NAVAJO STEW

2 lbs. ground beef
(browned & drained)

Season with cumin and
lemon pepper, to taste

Add and simmer:
2 cans whole kernel
corn (drained)
2 cans pinto beans
(undrained)
2 cans hominy (drained)
2 cans chopped stewed
tomatoes
2 small cans chopped
green chilies
6-10 cups chicken broth (or as much as needed).

Serve with grated cheese and sliced green onions.

(To increase amount, add 3 lbs. ground beef, 3 cans of everything. Can use black bean/pinto combination – improvise!)

Glenda Cotham

POTATO SOUP

3 c. chicken broth
2 onions – boil in broth
Boil 6-8 medium potatoes in broth.

Remove potatoes and onion. Place in blender or food processor with a little broth. Puree until liquid. Return potato mixture to broth. Add 2 c. milk, 2 tbsp. butter or margarine , and salt and pepper to taste.

To thicken, add 2 tbsp. flour mixed with ½ c. broth and return to broth. For variations, put cooked bacon/ham in soup and let simmer to add flavor (may be put in broth at beginning). Add cheese and crumble bacon bits to each bowl.

Karen Baxter

POTATO SOUP

½ stick oleo
1/8 tsp. pepper
2 tbsp. chopped onion
4 c. milk
1 ½ tsp. salt
¼ tsp. celery salt
3 medium potatoes
2 tbsp. flour

Peel and cube potatoes. Chop onions. Cover potatoes and onions with enough water to cook (about 15 minutes). Add oleo, celery salt, salt and pepper. Add flour to milk and add to the potato mixture. Heat to boiling, stirring occasionally.

Frances Johnson

SEA FOOD GUMBO

2 medium onions
2 cloves garlic
1 large can tomatoes
3 lbs. shelled shrimp
2 tsp. file` **
(** necessity)
2 medium bell peppers
2 pkg. cut frozen okra
2 cans crabmeat
2 tsp. thyme
salt & pepper to taste

Make roux in large boiler of 4 tablespoons fat and 1 tablespoon flour. Cook until dark brown. Chop onions, bell peppers, and garlic and soften in roux. Add ½ boiler hot water and frozen okra until soft. Use enough hot water to make a thick roux. Add tomatoes and simmer for 1 hour. Add crabmeat, shelled shrimp, thyme, salt, pepper, and file` and simmer again.

Cook 2 boxes wild rice. Put rice in bottom of soup bowls and ladle gumbo over rice. Serves 8.

Wanda Luna

TACO SOUP

2 lbs. ground chuck
1 can chili hot beans
1 can hominy
3 cans Mexican style tomatoes
1 pkg. Taco season mix
1 pkg. Hidden Valley Ranch dressing mix
1 chopped onion
1 can kidney beans
1 can corn niblets
1 can green chilies
2-3 cans of water

Brown meat and onions. Add all others (do not drain). Cook 45 minutes.

Carole Akin

TACO SOUP

Brown 1 lb. ground round, 1 chopped onion, and ¼ c. chopped green pepper.

Add:
1 can corn
1 can pinto beans
1 pkg. taco seasoning
2 cans stewed tomatoes
1 can ranch-style beans
1 can Coke
1 pkg. dry ranch dressing
16 oz. water
Salt, pepper, garlic powder, cayenne pepper to taste

Simmer one hour. Serve with grated cheddar cheese, tortilla chips and sour cream.

Faye Harlin

VEGETABLE CHEESE SOUP

1 c. chopped onion
2 c. coarsely chopped cabbage
1 c. sliced carrots
1 c. diced potatoes
¼ c. butter
3 c. milk
¼ tsp. paprika
¼ tsp. pepper (red or black)
2 tbsp. butter
1 (10 oz.) pkg. frozen baby lima beans
2 c. chicken broth
¼ c. flour
1 ½ c. (6 oz.) sharp cheese, shredded

Saute onion in 2 tbsp. butter; add cabbage, lima beans, carrots, potatoes and chicken broth.

Cover and simmer for 20 minutes or until tender.

Melt ¼ c. butter over low heat; add flour and cook 1 minute, stirring constantly.

Gradually add milk; cook over medium heat until thick.

Stir in cheese, paprika, and pepper. Stir cheese sauce into vegetables.

Serve soup immediately. Serves 8.

"Mystery Chef"

WHITE TURKEY CHILI

2 tbsp. olive oil
3 cloves garlic, minced
2 c. cooked, shredded turkey
1 ½ tbsp. chili powder
2 c. chicken broth
3 c. corn
2 cans white beans, mashed and drained
1 onion, chopped
3 tbsp. cumin
3 tsp. oregano
2 cans chopped green chiles, drained
chopped fresh cilantro
shredded Monterey Jack cheese and sour cream for garnish

Saute onion and garlic until clear and tender. Add in turkey, spices, and chiles and sauté until well mixed (2-3 minutes). Add chicken broth, corn and beans to pan. Bring to boil. Simmer uncovered for 1 hour. Mix with cilantro when serving. Top with cheese and sour cream, if desired.

Teresa & Chuck Fann

SWEET STUFF

CAKES

Notes...

APPLESAUCE CAKE

½ c. shortening
1 c. sugar
1 egg
1 c. applesauce
2 c. sifted flour
1 tsp. soda
1 tsp. salt
1 tsp. baking powder
1 tsp. cinnamon
½ tsp. allspice
½ tsp. nutmeg
¼ tsp. cloves
¾ c. nuts

Cream together the shortening and sugar; add egg and applesauce and beat well. Sift dry ingredients together; add to mixture.. Add nuts. Place in greased 8-inch pan and bake at 350 degrees for 50 to 60 minutes. Good with powdered sugar frosting.

Fae Holt

APPLESAUCE OR BANANA CAKE

½ c. butter
1 ½ c. sugar
3 eggs
1 ½ c. applesauce
 or 2 c. mashed bananas
½ tsp. nutmeg
1 c. raisins
½ tsp. salt
2 c. flour
2 tsp. soda
1 tsp. cinnamon
½ tsp. cloves
1 c. strawberry preserves
½ c. nuts (optional)

Grease 9 x 13 inch pan. Preheat oven to 325 degrees. Cream butter and sugar. Add eggs; beat until fluffy. Add raisins and nuts, if used.. Add alternately with applesauce or bananas and preserves to creamed mixture and mix well.
Pour into pan and bake for one hour or until done. Serve warm or cold with whipped topping and a cherry.

Eileen Moody

APRICOT NECTAR CAKE

1 box Duncan Hines Lemon Supreme cake mix
4 eggs
¾ c. apricot nectar
¾ c. Wesson oil

Mix well. Pour into stem pan and bake at 300 degrees for 1 hour.

ICING:

½ c. orange juice
2 c. powdered sugar, sifted

Mix and put on cake while warm. Let cake sit in pan until it is cooled.

Cheryl Wilson

BEE CAKE

(Very old German recipe from my great grandmother)

1 c. sugar
1 c. Presto flour

2 eggs in measuring cup – then fill cup to 1 cup mark with heavy cream. Mix all ingredients and bake in flat pan at 350 degrees until brown.

Toasted coconut topping:

5 tbsp. brown sugar
2 tbsp. butter
3 tbsp. light cream
¾ package coconut

Mix above in iron pan, apply to top of cake and broil in broiler until topping is brown. Cool to room temperature and serve.

Dr. Irene Ludwig Cox

BLACKBERRY JAM CAKE

1 c. butter
2 c. sugar
6 eggs
3 c. flour
½ c. buttermilk
2 c. blackberry jam
2 c. black walnuts, broken
1 tsp. salt
2 tsp. soda
1 tsp. nutmeg
1 tsp. cloves
1 tsp. cinnamon
2 c. raisins

Cream butter and sugar. Add eggs one at a time, beating after each. Mix together flour, salt and spices. Mix one cup flour mixture with nuts and raisins. Add soda to buttermilk. Add flour mixture and buttermilk to creamed butter-sugar-egg mixture, alternately. Fold in jam and raisin mixture. Use 2 -3 bundt pans or 3 or 4 loaf pans. Grease pan and flour. May use parchment paper in bottom. Bake at 350 degrees for 20 minutes. Reduce to 250 degrees and bake until done (20-40 minutes).

Charlotte Baskin

BUTTERMILK POUND CAKE

1 c. butter, softened
4 eggs
½ tsp. baking powder
1 tsp. vanilla
2 c. sugar
3 c. all purpose flour
1 c. buttermilk

Cream butter, gradually add sugar, beating at medium speed with electric mixer until blended. Add eggs one at a time. Combine flour and baking powder alternately with buttermilk, beginning and ending with flour mixture. Stir in flavoring.

Pour batter into a greased and floured 10 inch pan. Bake at 325 degrees for 1 hour or until a wooden toothpick inserted comes out clean. Remove from pan. Cool on rack. Very Good!

Juanita Goins

CARROT CAKE

2 c. sugar
4 eggs
2 tsp. soda
2 tsp. cinnamon
1 c. chopped nuts (opt.)
1 ½ c. cooking oil
2 c. flour
1 tsp. salt
3-4 c. grated carrots

Cream sugar and cooking oil. Add 4 eggs. Sift dry ingredients and add to sugar mixture. Add carrots and chopped nuts. The more carrots you add, the more moist the cake.)

Pour into 2 greased 9 inch pans or 9 x 13 inch sheet pan. Bake at 300 degrees for 1 hour. Let cool on wire rack.

ICING:

Cream 6-8 oz. cream cheese with ¾ stick butter. Add powdered sugar to taste. Then add 2 tsp. vanilla and ½ c. chopped nuts (optional).

Adjust amount of cream cheese and butter to your preference for thickness of icing.

(This has been a family favorite for decades.)

Ann Little

CHERRIES IN THE SNOW CAKE

Angel Food cake, broken up
½ c. powdered sugar
1 can cherry pie filling
8 oz. cream cheese
16 oz. Cool Whip

Mix powdered sugar, cream cheese and Cool Whip together. Layer cake, pie filling, and Cool Whip mixture. Repeat layers and place stemmed cherries on top. Pecans may be added. Place in deep dish, cover and refrigerate.

Jane DeFord

CHOCOLATE CAKE

1 box Duncan Hines Chocolate Fudge cake (butter recipe)
1 can cherry pie filling
2 eggs

Mix and bake at 350 degrees for 30 to 35 minutes. (Test with toothpick – cake is very moist.)

While cake is baking:
In saucepan, mix 1/3 cup milk, 5 tbsp. margarine, and 1 cup powdered sugar. Bring to a boil, and add 6 oz. chocolate chips. Beat with mixer until smooth.

Take cake out of oven and pour icing over cake while cake and icing are hot.

Frankie Reed

CINNAMON CAKE

1 box yellow cake mix (without pudding mix added)
1 package (3.4 oz.) vanilla instant pudding
3 eggs
2/3 c. oil
1 c. water
1 tsp. butter flavoring
1 tsp. vanilla flavoring
Mix together and beat 5-6 minutes.

NUT MIXTURE:
½ c. sugar
2 tsp. cinnamon
¼ c. chopped nuts

Mix together and alternate layers (3 batter and 2 nut mixture) beginning and ending with batter in a greased and floured tube pan. Bake at 350 degrees for 40-60 minutes.

Prepare glaze:
1 c. powdered sugar
3 tbsp. milk
½ tsp. butter
½ tsp. vanilla

Pour glaze over hot cake while still in pan. Cool and remove from pan.

Jane Guinn

COCONUT CAKE

Prepare 1 box white cake mix as directed. Pour into oblong pan. When done, poke holes in cake. Pour the following mixture over cake while warm:

1 can Lopez Cream of Coconut
1 can Eagle Brand milk.

Ice with Cool Whip when cake cools. Add sugar to fresh or frozen coconut and sprinkle on top

Darithy Baker

COCONUT POUND CAKE

2 c. sugar
2 c. self-rising flour
1 tsp. vanilla
½ c. whole milk
1 c. flaked coconut
1 c. oil
5 medium eggs
1 tsp. coconut flavoring

GLAZE:

2 tbsp. coconut flavoring
1/2 c. butter
1 c. sugar
½ c. water

Preheat oven to 350 degrees.

Mix sugar and oil together. Add eggs one at a time, beating after each. Add coconut, vanilla and coconut flavoring. Mix well. Add flour. Mix well. Add milk. Mix well. Bake in a tube pan with wax paper on the bottom (cutting a piece of wax paper in circle with hole in it to fit just the bottom of the pan.) Bake for 1 hour. While baking the cake make glaze. Combine all ingredients together in a pan and bring to a boil. Remove from heat.

Remove cake from oven and poke holes in the cake while still in the pan. Pour warm glaze onto the warm cake that is still in the pan. Let cool for 20-30 minutes before removing from pan. Peel off wax paper.

Janet Carell

COOKIE CAKE

1 box yellow cake mix
1 egg, slightly beaten
1 can Eagle Brand milk
1 (12 oz.) bag chocolate chips
1 c. chopped pecans
½ bag Heath Bits-O-Brickle

Combine milk and egg. Add cake mix and chopped pecans. Pour into pan and top with chocolate chips and Bits-O-Brickle. Bake at 350 degrees for 30-35 minutes. Tastes better if you let set a day.

Kevin Courtois

FRUIT COCKTAIL CAKE

1 medium can fruit cocktail
2 c. flour
1 tsp. soda
2 c. sugar
2 eggs

Mix all above ingredients together. Bake 45 min. at 350 degrees.

Topping:
2/3 c. sugar
1 stick butter
2/3 c. milk

Boil for 4 minutes. Add small can coconut and spread on top of cake.

Barbara Holt

HERSHEY'S SYRUP CAKE (AUNT MARTHA McPHERSON'S)

1/2 c. butter
1 c. sugar
4 eggs
1 ½ c. chocolate syrup
1 tsp. vanilla flavoring
1 c. plain flour
½ tsp. baking powder

Preheat oven to 350 degrees. Grease and flour a 9x13 inch pan. Cream butter and sugar. Add eggs, syrup, vanilla flavoring, flour and baking powder. Mix well. Bake for 25-30 minutes.

FROSTING:
½ c. butter
4 tbsp. cocoa
6 tbsp. milk
1 (1 lb.) box confectioners sugar
1 tsp. vanilla or almond flavoring

Melt butter in saucepan and add cocoa and milk. Stir and bring to a boil over medium heat. Take off stove and add flavoring and slowly add confectioners sugar beating with electric hand mixer.

DeLacy Bellenfant-Layhew

JAM CAKE & CARAMEL ICING

2 c. sugar
6 eggs
½ c. shortening
1 c. nuts
1 tsp. cinnamon
1 tsp. allspice
1 tsp. salt
1 lb. crystalized cherries
1 lb. crystalized pineapple
4 c. flour
1 c. buttermilk
2 c. jam
2 c. raisins
1 tsp. nutmeg
2 tsp. soda

Cream shortening and sugar. Add jam. Add dry ingredients alternately with buttermilk. Then add nuts, raisins, and crystalized fruit. Put in two 9x9x1 ¾ inch cake pans and cook 2 hours at 275 degrees.

CARAMEL ICING:

3 c. sugar
1 ½ c. cream
1 tsp. vanilla
2 tbsp. syrup
¼ tsp. baking powder

Caramelize ½ c. sugar. Mix other sugar in saucepan with the cream, syrup, and baking powder. When sugar is caramelized, mix together. Cook until a soft ball is formed in cold water. Add vanilla and beat. Spread on cake.

Annie Lillard

LEMON LOAF CAKE

4 eggs (or 1 egg
 and 4 egg whites)
½ c. Crisco
¼ tsp. salt
¼ tsp. soda
1 c. buttermilk
2 ¼ c. flour
2 ¼ c. sugar
½ c. margarine
2 tsp. lemon or vanilla extract
1 tsp. baking powder

Cream Crisco and margarine with sugar. Beat in eggs one at a time. Sift dry ingredients and add to creamed mixture alternately with buttermilk. Add lemon or vanilla extract. Bake 50-60 minutes at 350 degrees.

Karen Morris

MANDARIN ORANGE CAKE

1 box Duncan Hines
 Moist Deluxe cake mix
1 – 11 oz. can mandarin
 oranges (drained)
4 whole eggs
¾ c. Wesson Oil

Mix all the above and beat for 2 minutes. (If too stiff, put some of drained orange juice in batter.) Pour into 3 greased and floured 9 inch round pans. Bake in 350 degree oven for 20 minutes. When cool, cover layers with icing and refrigerate in covered cake container. Better the next day!

ICING:
1 carton Cool Whip (9 oz.)
1 small box instant
 French Vanilla pudding mix
1 can crushed drained
 pineapple (13 oz.)

Dot Baxter

MANDARIN ORANGE CAKE

1 box yellow cake mix
1 can mandarin oranges (do not drain)

Mix cake as directed on box – omit water.

Icing:

Mix together 1 carton of Cool Whip, 1 small can crushed pineapple (do not drain), and 1 box vanilla instant pudding. Keep in refrigerator. This makes a cool summer dessert!

Anne Cherry

MILLION DOLLAR POUND CAKE

3 c. sugar
¾ c. milk
1 tsp. vanilla
1 tsp. almond flavoring
1 lb. soft butter
6 eggs (room temperature)
4 c. all purpose flour

Combine sugar and butter. Cream until light and fluffy. Add eggs, one at a time – beating well after each addition. Add flour to creamed mixture alternately with milk, beating well after each addition. Stir in flavorings.

Pour batter into well-greased and floured 10-inch tube pan. Bake at 300 degrees for 1 hr. and 40 minutes or until cake tests done. Let stand 30 minutes before removing from pan. If there are leftovers, this is delicious for breakfast! Slice and run in oven under broiler until both sides are toasty!

Anita Anderson

OATMEAL CAKE

Pour 1 ½ cups of boiling water over a cup of oatmeal and let stand for 20 minutes.

Add:

½ c. shortening or oil
1 ½ c. flour
2 eggs
1 tsp. soda
1 tsp. vanilla
1 c. brown sugar
1 c. white sugar
1 tsp. salt
1 tsp. cinnamon

Mix well and bake in a 9 x 13 inch pan for 30-35 minutes at 350 degrees.

TOPPING:

½ c. brown sugar
½ tsp. vanilla
½ stick butter
¼ c. canned milk
1 c. nuts

Mix well. Spread on cake. Put under broiler for 3-4 minutes. Watch – it burns easily!

"Mystery Chef"

SCRUMPTIOUS STRAWBERRY SURPRISE

1 Duncan Hines yellow cake mix
4 boxes frozen, sweetened strawberries
2 cartons whipping cream

Thaw strawberries. Bake cake as directed on box in 2 round cake pans. Let cool. Pour strawberries between each layer and on the top layer. Make sure cake is saturated with all strawberry juice. Put in refrigerator overnight. Prepare whipping cream and cover entire cake. Um, Um – good!

Nelda Bates

SOUR CREAM POUND CAKE

1 box Duncan Hines Butter Recipe Golden cake mix
½ c. oil
1 tbsp. vanilla flavoring
4 eggs
¾ c. sugar
8 oz. sour cream

Mix all ingredients until smooth. Spray bundt cake pan – add ingredients. Cook at 325 degrees for 45-50 minutes. Sprinkle with confectioners sugar.

Sherry Shouse

STRAWBERRY CAKE

1 large box frozen strawberries
4 eggs
strawberry juice (or water) from frozen strawberries
1 box white cake mix
2/3 c. vegetable oil
1 small box strawberry jello

Thaw strawberries. Drain – save juice. Mix cake mix and jello together. Add I cup strawberry juice. Add vegetable oil and eggs. Beat until smooth. Bake 2 layers at 350 degrees for approximately 30 minutes or until done. Let cool completely before icing.

Icing:
1 box confectioners sugar
red food color – approx. 6 drops
2 packages cream cheese

Beat all ingredients together. Add few drops of strawberry juice, a little at a time, until you have the right consistency. Ice bottom layer and place mashed strawberries over bottom layer. Put top layer on and cover with icing.

Teresa Perry

SUNDROP CAKE

lemon cake mix
12 oz. Sundrop
¼ c. oil
lemon pudding
3 eggs

Mix all ingredients well – bake in bundt pan sprayed with Pam. Cook 45 minutes at 350 degrees. Cool 15 – 20 minutes in pan.

GLAZE:
1 c. powdered sugar
1 tsp. vanilla flavoring
2 tbsp. lemon juice
Mix until smooth and drizzle over cake.

Lynn Babcock

VANILLA WAFER CAKE

1 box vanilla wafers (crushed)
1 c. coconut
2 c. sugar
½ c. milk
1 ½ sticks melted butter
6 eggs, beaten
1 c. chopped pecans

Mix all above ingredients. Grease bundt pan and sprinkle with flour. Heat oven to 350 degrees and bake for 1-1 ½ hours.

ICING:

1 box powdered sugar. Start with ½ box and add.
1 – 8 oz. cream cheese
½ stick butter
1 tsp. vanilla flavoring

Mix together and pour on cake.

Tiffany Richmond
(Our daughter)

SWEET STUFF

CANDY & BROWNIES

Notes...

BROWN SUGAR BROWNIES

2 sticks margarine
1 tsp. baking powder
4 eggs
¼ tsp. salt
3 c. or 1 lb. brown sugar
2 tsp. vanilla
2 c. flour

Cream sugar and margarine. Add remaining ingredients. Bake at 325 degrees for 40 minutes.

Linda Cotton

BUTTERSCOTCH BROWNIES

¼ c. butter, soft shortening, or vegetable oil
1 egg
1 tsp. baking powder
½ tsp. vanilla
1 c. light brown sugar (packed)
¾ c. sifted flour
½ tsp. salt
½ c. coarsely chopped nuts

Heat oven to 350 degrees. Melt shortening over low heat. Remove from heat. Stir in sugar until blended. Cool. Stir in egg. Sift together flour, baking powder and salt; stir in. Mix in vanilla and nuts. Spread in well greased square pan 8 x 8 x 2 inches. Bake 25 minutes. DO NOT OVERBAKE. Cut into bars while warm. Makes 18 bars. (I always double recipe). These chewy bars keep deliciously soft for days in tightly covered jar. They also freeze well.

Martha Adams

BUTTERSCOTCH BROWNIES

1 box light or dark brown sugar
2 sticks margarine (melted)
1 tsp. vanilla
½ c. white sugar
4 eggs (beaten)
2 ¼ c. self-rising flour
1 c. chopped pecans

Put brown sugar and margarine in bowl. Add eggs. Beat well, then add white sugar, flour, vanilla and nuts. Bake at 350 degrees in large oven pan for about 25-35 minutes. Let sit and then sprinkle with confectioners sugar and cut in squares.

Clarice Collins

CHERRY DELIGHT

(Double Recipe)

1. Place 12 double graham crackers, rolled in ¼ cup margarine and 2 tbsp. powdered sugar, in a large baking dish. Bake at 350 degrees for 10 minutes.

2. Prepare mixture of 1 large package cream cheese mixed with enough milk to desired consistency. Spread over crackers and sprinkle with 1 cup nuts.

3. Cover with prepared cherry or blueberry pie filling.

4. Whip 1 pint whipping cream with 1 tbsp. sugar and 2 tsp. vanilla and spread on top.

Lois Swords

CHESS CAKE SQUARES

2 sticks real butter
¾ c. sugar
½ tsp. vanilla
1 c. chopped pecans
1 box light brown sugar
4 eggs
2 c. self-rising flour

Spray 9 x 13 inch pan with Pam. Preheat oven to 350 degrees. Melt butter in pan on stove top. Add both sugars and eggs, one at a time, beating after each. Fold in flour and nuts. Add vanilla. Pour mixture in pan and bake 40 minutes. Sift powdered sugar on top.

Karen Pratt

CHOCOLATE BROWNIES

Prepare 1 box Betty Crocker family style brownie mix as directed on box. Pour ½ of the brownie mix in baking dish and put 3 Symphony Hershey candy bars (almond and toffee) side by side on top. Cover with the remaining brownie mix. Bake in a 13 x 9 inch glass dish in middle of the oven at 350 degrees for 30 minutes. Cool. Cut into squares. Makes 24 large or 42 small squares.

Carol Gammon

CRANBERRY-APPLE CRISP

3 c. chopped apples
1 c. granulated sugar
½ c. chopped pecans
1 c. quick oats
2 c. whole raw cranberries
½ c. brown sugar
1 stick butter or margarine, cut in small pieces

Spread apples and cranberries in a buttered 2-quart dish. Spread sugars, oats and nuts over apples and cranberries. Top with butter. Bake for 1 hour at 325 degrees. Good with vanilla ice cream.

Christy Wampler

GOOEY BUTTER BARS

1 box yellow cake mix
1 stick margarine or butter (melted)
1 egg
1 c. chopped nuts

Mix above and pat evenly in 13 x 9 inch pan.

TOPPING:
1 pkg. (8 oz.) cream cheese (softened)
1 box powdered sugar
2 eggs

Mix topping ingredients in mixer until well blended. Pour over bottom layer. Bake at 350 degrees for 45 minutes. Cut in squares after completely cooled.

Rosemary Smithson

IRISH POTATO CANDY

(My grandmother, Lucy Shaw, taught me this and we made it together on many Christmases. Her mother taught it to her – so it's an <u>old</u> recipe.)

1 medium Irish potato
Smooth peanut butter
2 boxes confectioners sugar

Peel and boil potato, drain water off. Slowly add confectioners sugar. Should be firm and "doughy". Sprinkle some of the sugar on wax paper and spread the potato sugar mixture on it. Then spread with a layer of smooth peanut butter. Roll whole thing up like a log and wrap in Saran Wrap. Refrigerate. Slice when ready to use. Will look like pinwheel. Very delicious! Makes 2-3 logs.

Sherry Bellenfant

LEMON SQUARES

CRUST:

1 c. flour
¼ tsp. salt
½ c. butter
¼ c. powdered sugar

Mix together and bake in a 9x9 inch pan at 350 degrees for 20 minutes.

FILLING:

1 c. sugar
½ tsp. baking powder
3 tbsp. lemon juice
3 tbsp. flour
2 eggs, beaten

Sift dry ingredients together and combine with the eggs and lemon juice. Pour over hot crust. Bake at 350 degrees for 20 minutes.

(Three recipes makes 70 small squares in long Teflon pan. Sprinkle with confectioners sugar or cut in large squares and serve with whipped cream and twist of lemon.)

Christi Smith
(our daughter)

PEANUT BUTTER FUDGE

3 c. sugar
1 tbsp. butter
¾ c. milk
6 ½ oz. marshmallow cream
1 tsp. vanilla
2 tbsp. cocoa
12 oz. peanut butter

Mix sugar, vanilla, butter, cocoa and milk together and boil 3 minutes. Remove from heat and add marshmallow cream and peanut butter. Mix well and pour into a buttered pan. Let cool – cut and serve!

Mandy Davis

PEANUT BUTTER RICE CRISPIES

1 c. sugar
1 c. peanut butter
1 c. milk chocolate chips
1 c. light corn syrup
6 c. Rice Krispies
1 c. butterscotch chips

Mix sugar and corn syrup and bring to a boil. Remove from heat. Add peanut butter and mix well. Add Rice Krispies until coated. Spread in 9 x 13 inch pan. Melt chocolate and butterscotch chips. Spread over Rice Krispie mix and let cool.

Julie Bickmore

SOUTH KENTUCKY FUDGE

1 c. buttermilk or sour cream
2 c. sugar
1 tsp. vanilla
1 tsp. soda
2 tbsp. butter

Combine soda with buttermilk in 4 qt. saucepan. Let stand 5 minutes. Stir in sugar gradually. Continue to stir over medium heat until dissolved. Insert candy thermometer. Add butter and cook, occasionally stirring until thermometer registers 232 degrees or until soft ball stage. Remove from heat. Let cool. Do not stir. Add vanilla. Beat until it begins to hold. Pour in buttered plate.

Mildred Elliott

SUNBURST MUFFINS

1 box Lemon Supreme cake mix
½ c. vegetable oil
4 eggs
1 pkg. lemon instant pudding mix (3 ¾ oz.)
1 c. buttermilk

Mix all the above together. Pour into muffin tins and bake at 350 degrees. When done, and while warm, dip top of the muffin in glaze:

3 tbsp. fresh lemon juice
1 ½ tsp. vanilla flavoring
6 tbsp. fresh orange juice
3 ½ c. powdered sugar

Cool on rack. YUM!! YUM!!

Betty Ladd

SWEET STUFF

ICE CREAM & COOKIES

Notes...

HOMEMADE ICE CREAM

(Given to me by my mother)

2 c. sugar
½ gal. whole milk
(add more to fill freezer)
dash of salt
vanilla flavoring
4 eggs
2 pt. whipping cream
(to your mark on freezer)
Junket tablets

4 Junket tablets dissolved in 1 tbsp. of water. Set aside to dissolve. Mix sugar, eggs, milk, whipping cream, and salt. Warm on stove or microwave until lukewarm. Remove and add dissolved Junket tablets to mixture. Add vanilla. Place mixture into freezer and let set 10 minutes. Then freeze with salt and ice.

If you want to add fruit, adjust sugar. Add fruit after mixture has been heated. Allow room in freezer for fruit. Freezes much better leaving plenty room.

Barbara Knight

HOMEMADE VANILLA ICE CREAM

4 eggs
2 tsp. vanilla
1 pt. whipping cream
2 c. sugar
1 qt. Half & Half
fill with whole milk

Beat eggs and add sugar. Combine remaining ingredients. Put in freezer and fill remainder of freezer with whole milk to within 1 inch of the top.

Tommy McArthur
(our son)

ORANGE-PINEAPPLE ICE CREAM

Mix one box 6 oz. orange jello with 2 c. boiling water and set aside.

4 eggs
1 can crushed pineapple (20 oz.)
1 can evaporated milk (13 oz.)
1 carton Cool Whip (8 oz.)
1 ½ c. sugar
1 can sweetened condensed milk (14 oz.)
frozen orange juice (6 oz.)

Mix all together, finish filling freezer with milk.

Ruth Edmondson

PEACH ICE CREAM (MAMMAW'S)

1 can Eagle Brand milk
1 ½ c. sugar
1 qt. peaches
1 large can Pet Milk (2 c.)
4 eggs, beaten
milk to finish

Beat eggs and sugar. Combine with rest of ingredients. Put in freezer and fill remainder of freezer with whole milk to within 1 inch of the top.

Tommy McArthur
(our son)

ROBERT'S PEACH ICE CREAM

6 eggs
3 c. sugar
2 qts. Half & Half
½ tsp. salt
1 tbsp. pure vanilla extract
5 c. ripe peaches (peeled, seeded & sweetened to taste)
Whole milk to fill to 1 ½ inches below top of freezer can.

In a large mixing bowl, beat eggs until fluffy. Add sugar a little at a time, beating continuously. When sugar and eggs are beaten together, add salt, vanilla and 1 qt. of the Half & Half. Blend peaches in a blender until smooth and add to the custard mix. Pour into freezer can, add the second qt. of Half & Half and enough milk to fill to within 1 ½ inches below the top of freezer can.

Place in freezer tub and freeze as usual Makes 6 quarts/1 ½ gallon.

Better if frozen 2-3 hours before serving and packed or wrapped in several layers to insulate.

NOTE: Remove dasher before packing.

Robert Davis

CANDIED FRUIT COOKIES (CHRISTMAS)

1 c. margarine /butter (softened)
1 c. powdered sugar
2 ½ c. all-purpose flour
1 egg
¼ tsp. cream of tartar
½ c. chopped pecans (I use 1 cup)
½ c. chopped mixed candied fruit
1 c. candied whole cherries

Mix butter, sugar and egg. Stir in remaining ingredients. Divide dough in half and shape into roll – 1 ½ inches diameter. Wrap and chill at least 4 hours. (I put mine in the freezer and use later).

Thaw before slicing in 1/8 inch slices. Place 1 inch apart on ungreased baking sheet. Bake about 8 minutes at 375 degrees. Makes 6 dozen.

(This recipe was given to me years ago by my dear fried, Corinne Jones, who taught Home Economics at Franklin HS for 30 years.)

Sarah W. Jordan

MAMA'S TEACAKES

1 c. Crisco
2 c. sugar
3 eggs
¼ tsp. soda
1 ½ tsp. vanilla
¼ c. milk
4 c. flour
½ tsp. salt
1 tsp. baking powder

Cream sugar and Crisco. Beat eggs into it – then add milk. Add dry ingredients together. Add dry ingredients to wet ingredients. Let dough sit in refrigerator 2-3 hours. Bake at 400 degrees until brown. Delicious as soon as they come out of oven!

Marie Jordan

MA'S LACE COOKIES

(My 99 ½ year old grandmother's, Lucy Shaw, recipe)

3 tbsp. sugar
3 tbsp. butter
2 tbsp. light molasses (Karo)
¼ tsp. water

Mix and bring to a boil. Add:

1 1/3 c. sifted flour
½ tsp. cinnamon
¼ c. chopped nuts
½ tsp. baking powder
salt to taste

Stir until blended. Drop 1 tbsp. of mixture on well greased cookie sheet, spread thin as possible. Bake several at one time. Cool slightly and shape into cones or fan. Bake at 325 degrees for 9-10 minutes.

Emy Joe Bellenfant- Bilbrey

MRS. FIELD'S COOKIES

2 c. butter
2 c. brown sugar
2 tsp. vanilla
5 c. oatmeal (blend in blender for oat flour)
2 tsp. baking powder
8 oz. Hershey bar, grated
2 c. sugar
4 eggs
4 c. flour
3 c. nuts
2 tsp. baking soda
24 oz. bag chocolate chips
3 c. nuts

Mix all ingredients and shape into golf ball size. Space 2 inches apart. Bake at 375 degrees for 6 minutes. Yields approximately 112 cookies.

Heidi and Carl Wallace

PEANUT BUTTER CHOCOLATE OATMEAL COOKIES

½ c. cocoa
½ c. butter
½ c. milk
2 c. sugar

Bring these 4 ingredients to a rolling boil in a skillet and boil for 1 minute. In a bowl have 3 cups of oats and ½ cup of peanut butter prepared. Pour in cooked mixture, stir well and drop by spoonfuls onto waxed paper. "Eat when cool!"

Dawn Moss

PECAN CRESCENTS

1 c. butter (no substitute) softened
2 ½ c. flour, sifted several times
4 tbsp. confectioners' sugar
1 c. pecans, finely chopped

Beat butter and sugar until creamy. Add flour. Stir in pecans. Use rounded teaspoons of dough and shape into crescents. Place on ungreased cookie sheet. Bake at 250 degrees for 50 minutes. Cool and roll in powdered sugar.

Mary Wheeler

SORGHUM GINGERSNAPS

2 c. sugar
1 c. shortening
2 eggs
½ c. sorghum or mild molasses
3 ½ c. all-purpose flour
2 tsp. ground ginger
1 ½ tsp. ground cinnamon
1 tsp. ground cloves
2 tsp. baking soda

Preheat oven to 350 degrees. In a large mixing bowl beat the sugar and shortening with an electric mixer on medium speed until fluffy. Beat in eggs and sorghum. Stir together flour, baking soda, ginger, cinnamon and cloves. Gradually beat or stir flour mixture into beaten mixture. Shape dough into 1 inch balls; roll in additional sugar. Place on ungreased cookie sheet. Bake 12 minutes or until bottoms are lightly browned. Cool on racks. Makes about 7 dozen cookies.

Hayley Preston

SPECIAL K COOKIES

1 c. white sugar
1 c. white syrup
1-13 oz. jar peanut butter
1 c. coconut
½ c. brown sugar
1 tsp. vanilla
1 c. roasted peanuts
5 c. Special K cereal

Combine sugar with syrup in a sauce pan. Bring to a rolling boil. Do not over-cook. Remove from heat. Add peanut butter and vanilla and beat until smooth. Mix nuts, coconut and Special K together in large bowl. Combine both mixtures and mix thoroughly. Drop on wax paper by spoonful or roll in balls.

Hazeline Pratt

THE BEST OATMEAL & SOUR CREAM CHOCOLATE CHIP COOKIE

2 c. flour
1 tsp. baking soda
½ tsp. salt
1 c. rolled oats
1 ¼ c. light brown sugar
2 eggs
1 c. unsalted butter, softened
1 tsp. vanilla
½ c. sour cream
12-oz. pkg. semi-sweet chocolate chips
12-oz. pkg. milk chocolate chips
¼ c. raisins, coarsely chopped
¾ c. dried cherries or dried cranberries
¾ c. walnut or pecan pieces chopped

Sift together flour, baking soda and salt. Mix in rolled oats. Set aside. In large bowl, cream together sugar and butter. Beat in eggs and vanilla. Stir sifted ingredients into creamed mixture until just combined. Mix in sour cream and stir until blended. Add chocolate chips, raisins, dried cherries and nuts. Drop by heaping spoonfuls onto ungreased cookie sheets. Bake at 350 degrees for 12-15 minutes. Yields about 5 ½ dozen cookies.

Leah Karo

SWEET STUFF

PIES, PUDDING & TARTS

Notes...

APPLE DUMPLINGS

2 Granny Smith apples, peeled and cored
1 (8-count) can crescent rolls
1/8 tsp. cinnamon
½ c. butter or margarine
1 c. sugar
1 c. orange juice
1 tsp. vanilla

Cut apples into quarters. Unwrap and separate crescent rolls. Wrap a piece of apple in each roll. Place dumplings in 9-inch square baking dish and sprinkle with cinnamon. Combine butter, sugar and orange juice in saucepan and bring to a boil. Remove from heat and stir in vanilla. Pour over dumplings (syrup cooks down as dumplings bake). Bake at 350 degrees for 30 minutes. Spoon syrup over dumplings when serving.

Wanda Mahan

BANANAS FOSTER TART

CRUST: 1 Pillsbury refrigerated pie crust

FILLING:
2 medium bananas cut into ¼ inch thick slices
2/3 c. firmly packed brown sugar
¼ c. whipping cream
½ tsp. vanilla
4 ½ tsp. light rum*
2 tsp. grated orange peel
2/3 c. chopped pecans
¼ c. butter

TOPPING: vanilla ice cream, if desired

1. Heat oven to 450 degrees. Prepare pie crust as directed on package for one-crust **baked** shell using 9-inch tart pan with removable bottom or 9-inch pie pan. Place crust in pan; press in bottom and up sides. Trim edges, if necessary. Bake for 9 to 11 minutes or until light golden brown. Cool 5 minutes.

(Continued on next page)

2. In small bowl, combine bananas and rum; toss to coat. Sprinkle orange peel evenly in bottom of baked shell. Arrange bananas in single layer over peel. Sprinkle with pecans.
3. In heavy medium saucepan, combine brown sugar, whipping cream and butter; cook and stir over medium-high heat for 2 to 3 minutes or until mixture comes to a boil. Cook an additional 2 to 4 minutes or until mixture has thickened and is deep golden brown, stirring constantly.
4. Remove saucepan from heat; stir in vanilla. Spoon warm filling over bananas and pecans. Cool 30 minutes. Serve warm or cool with ice cream. Store in refrigerator. Serves 10.

TIP: *To substitute for rum, combine ½ tsp. rum extract with 4 tsp. water.

Pat Iannacone

BANANA PUDDING

¾ c. sugar
pinch of salt
1 egg
3 – 4 bananas
2 heaping tbsp. flour
1 c. milk
vanilla flavoring
vanilla wafers

Mix sugar, flour and salt together. Add egg and milk. Stir constantly over medium-high heat until your arms fall off or until thick (whichever happens first). Remove from heat and add one teaspoon of vanilla (not heaping).

Layer vanilla wafers, bananas and pudding in bowl and sprinkle with nutmeg on top if you wish.

Rynda McMurray

BANANA SPLIT PIE

1 Graham Cracker Crust Pie Shell
2 or 3 bananas (sliced length-wise)
1 small can crushed pineapple (drained)
1 large container Cool Whip
2 c. powdered sugar
2 egg whites
1 stick butter (melted)
2 c. powdered sugar
Small jar whole or sliced Maraschino cherries, (optional)

Beat together powdered sugar, egg whites and stick of melted butter. Mix thoroughly.

Peel and slice bananas length-wise down the middle of banana.

Layer the following in the Graham Cracker Crust Pie Shell in the order listed:

Layer 1: Powdered sugar / egg whites mix

Layer 2: Sliced bananas

Layer 3: Drained pineapple

Layer 4: Cool Whip

Cover completely with cherries, if desired. Refrigerate for 2 -3 hours. Keep refrigerated.

Faye Jones

BOURBON- CHOCOLATE PECAN PIE

1 9-inch unbaked pie crust
1 c. light corn syrup
½ c. sugar
3 tbsp. bourbon
1 tbsp. vanilla extract
1 c. semi-sweet chocolate chips
4 large eggs
6 tbsp. butter or oleo, melted
¼ c. packed brown sugar
1 tbsp. flour
1 c. coarsely chopped pecans

In a mixing bowl, whisk together the flour, sugar and brown sugar. Then add the eggs, light corn syrup, butter, bourbon and vanilla. Stir in the chopped pecans. Sprinkle the chocolate chips in the bottom of the pie shell and pour the pecan mixture on top.

Bake at 350 degrees for 1 hour or until set.

Nancy Moody

CHESS PIE

1 ½ c. sugar
3 eggs
2 tbsp. buttermilk
1 stick melted margarine
½ tsp. vinegar
1 ½ tsp. meal
1 tsp. vanilla

DO NOT PREHEAT OVEN!!

Beat eggs. Put sugar in eggs; add melted margarine. Beat by hand. Add remaining ingredients and beat again. Pour in unbaked pie shell and cook at 350 degrees for 30 minutes. Turn off oven and allow pie to continue cooking.

May put iron griddle under pie to bake evenly.

Carol Jenkins

CHESS PIE

Combine 1 ½ c. sugar and 1 tbsp. corn meal.

Add:
½ c. melted butter
1 tsp. vinegar
¼ c. milk
3 whole eggs, one at time
1 tsp. vanilla (add and stir)

Mix with a spoon and pour in unbaked pie shell. Bake at 400 degrees for 10 minutes, drop to 325 degrees for 30 minutes.

Jere Phillips

COCOLATE CHIP TARTS

chocolate chips, semi-sweet
4 eggs, beaten
1 c. white Karo syrup
1 stick melted butter
pecans
1 c. sugar
1 tsp. vanilla
2 pkg. frozen tarts -16

Combine sugar, eggs, syrup, vanilla and mix well. Melt butter. Add to mixture.

Place tarts on a cookie sheet. Add 7-10 chocolate chips in each tart. Add chopped pecans (even amount). Mix remaining ingredients and spoon into tarts.

Bake at 350 degrees for 30-35 minutes. Cool on rack.

Teresa & Chuck Fann

COCONUT CHESS PIE
(Makes 3 pies)

2 sticks margarine
2 c. sugar
1 ½ c. white karo
6 eggs
2 tsp. vanilla
2 2/3 c. coconut

Melt margarine. Add sugar and syrup. Mix in eggs that are well beaten. Add vanilla and coconut. Put 1 ½ c. mixture in each pie shell and then split up the rest.

Cook at 300 degrees for 1 hour. Cool before serving.

Paulette Coleman

COCONUT CREAM PIE

2 c. milk
1 tbsp. cornstarch
¼ tsp. salt
3 tbsp. flour
½ c. sugar
3 egg yolks

Put above ingredients in blender and mix well. Stir over medium heat then add:

1-2 tbsp. butter
1 c. coconut
1 tsp. vanilla

Pour in baked pie shell.

Meringue: 3 egg whites, ¼ c. sugar, vanilla

Bake at 350 degrees for 10 minutes.

Emy Joe Bellenfant- Bilbrey

CREAMY BANANA PUDDING

1 (14 oz.) can Eagle Brand sweetened condensed milk
3-4 bananas
1 (4 serving size) package instant vanilla pudding mix
vanilla wafers
1 ½ c. cold water
2 c. whipping cream (whipped)

In huge bowl combine Eagle Brand and water. Add pudding mix and beat well (2 minutes). Chill 5 minutes or more. Fold in whipped cream. Spoon 1 cup pudding mixture into 2 ½ quart glass serving bowl. Top with 1/3 each of the wafers, bananas and pudding. Repeat layering twice, ending with pudding. Chill thoroughly. 8-10 servings. Delicious!

Gayle Brinkley

FORGET IT TORTE

6 egg whites (room temperature)
1 tsp. vanilla
½ tsp. cream of tartar
1 ½ c. sugar (sifted)
¼ tsp. salt

Beat egg whites, cream of tartar, and salt until foamy. Add sugar gradually. Beat until very stiff. Add vanilla.

Butter bottom of spring type pan. Pour in mixture and put in 450 degree oven. Turn oven off immediately and leave in oven at least 8 hours. Ice torte with whipping cream and put strawberries or peaches on top. Keep in refrigerator until ready to serve.

Ruth Sewell

GRASSHOPPER PIE

1 c. chocolate chips
1 ½ c. chopped pecans
1/3 c. milk
3 tbsp. crème de menth
1 ½ c. whipped cream
1 tbsp. Crisco
½ lb. marshmallows
¼ tsp. salt
3 tbsp. white crème de cocoa
1 chocolate pie crust

Line a 9 inch pie plate with foil. Combine over hot water, chocolate and Crisco. Stir until smooth. Add nuts. Spread on bottom and sides of foil and refrigerate. Combine over hot water, marshmallows, milk and salt. Heat until melted. Remove from heat. Add liquors. Stir until blended. Chill for 1 hour. Gently fold in whipped cream. Pour in chocolate pie crust after removing foil.

Wanda Luna

HERSHEY BAR PIE

6 small Hershey bars (almond)
20 large marshmallows
1 Graham Cracker pie shell
¼ c. milk
1 c. whipping cream

Melt Hershey bars, marshmallows and milk on low heat. Cool. Mix 1 c. whipped cream into cooled chocolate mixture. Pour into graham cracker pie shell.

Esther Sitton

LAZY MAN'S PEACH PIE

1 stick butter
1 tsp. baking powder
1 can or 2 c. sliced peaches
(drain juice and reserve)
¾ c. milk
1 c. sugar
¾ c. flour

Melt butter in casserole dish. Mix dry ingredients together. Add milk and mix. Spread over butter. Pour peaches over this, leaving juice to be poured over all. Bake 40-45 minutes at 350 degrees.

(This recipe is in my first cookbook called Jeanne Pruett's Feedin' Friends on page 51. It's like magic. As the cobbler cooks, the crust oozes up and thru it to the top as it browns. (You will love it – I use it at least once a week.) Vanilla ice cream over it warm is wonderful!

Jeanne Pruett Fulton

LOW-CARB LEMON MERINGUE PIE

4 eggs, separated
2 c. boiling water
2 tbsp. butter or
1 stick margarine
3 tbsp. sugar for meringue
2 tbsp. Splenda for meringue
4 tbsp. cornstarch
1 ¼ c. Splenda
¾ c. lemon juice
dash salt (optional)
1 -9 inch pie crust, baked

Mix Splenda, egg yolks, lemon juice and cornstarch. Add boiling water and cook in double boiler, stirring until thick. Add butter and cool. Pour into baked pie crust. Beat egg whites, adding sugar and Splenda 2 tablespoons at a time. Add salt. Cover pie and brown in 400 degree oven for 10 minutes.

Note: You can use all Splenda in meringue, but it will be dry. I find by adding 3 tablespoons of each, you get a better meringue. If you are diabetic – adjust your carbs in the rest of your meal.

Evelyn Brewer

NANNY'S CREAM PIE

2/3 c. whipping cream
3 heaping tbsp. plain flour
½ stick oleo
1 c. sugar
1 tbsp. vanilla

Preheat oven to 300 degrees. Mix and bake 10 minutes. Turn oven up to 350 degrees until done.

Carolyn Lynch

PEAR DUMPLINGS

8 pears
1 stick butter
1 c. sugar
1 tsp. vanilla
2 pkg. crescent refrigerated rolls
1 c. orange juice

Peel pears and cut in half. Wrap each half in crescent roll.

Melt 1 stick of butter in a sauce pan. Add 1 cup sugar and 1 cup orange juice. Bring to boil. Let liquid get clear. Cool mixture and add 1 tsp. vanilla. Pour over pears. Bake at 350 degrees for 1 hour.

JoAnn Irwin

PECAN PIE

2/3 c. sugar
1/3 tsp. salt
1 c. pecans
1/3 c. melted butter
3 eggs

Beat with rotary beater and pour in unbaked pie shell. Put nuts on top. Bake at 375 degrees 40-50 minutes.

Elva Beard

PECAN PIE

1 9-inch unbaked pie crust

Mix:
½ c. sugar
1 c. pecan pieces
1 heaping tbsp. flour
1 tsp. vanilla
1 c. white corn syrup
4 tbsp. butter, chopped or melted
2 whole eggs

Pour into crust. Bake at 350 degrees for 45-50 minutes until brown.

Peggy Crockett

RIVERSTREET RESTAURANT PIE

1 box yellow cake mix
1 egg
1 stick butter
1 cup chopped nuts

Blend above ingredients in mixer. Put ½ mixture in each of 2 prepared pie shells.

TOPPING:
8 oz. cream cheese
1 lb. powdered sugar.
2 eggs
Mix together and pour over top of mixture.

Bake at 350 degrees for 45 min. – 1 hr. Serve warm. Top with vanilla bean ice cream.

Diane Bailey

THREE LAYER PIE

Layer 1:

1 ½ stick margarine
1 ½ c. plain flour
1 ½ c. chopped nuts

Melt margarine. Add flour and pecans. Mix well and press in a 9x13 inch pan or dish.

Bake about 30 minutes at 350 degrees or until medium brown. Store in refrigerator until completely cooled.

Layer 2:

8 oz. pkg. cream cheese
1 c. powdered sugar
1 c. Cool Whip

Mix cream cheese and sugar. Beat until fluffy. Fold in Cool Whip. Spread over first layer.

Layer 3:

2 small pkg. instant pudding
1 carton Cool Whip
3 ½ c. sweet milk

Mix 2 packages instant chocolate or butterscotch pudding with milk and beat until smooth. Let set for a while, then pour over second layer. Place in refrigerator. Top with Cool Whip.

Sue Dodd Locke

WILLIE MAE'S CHOCOLATE PIE

¾ stick butter, softened
pinch of salt
5 level tbsp. cocoa
vanilla flavoring
1 ½ c. sugar
3 beaten egg yolks
6 large tbsp. all purpose flour.

Mix butter, sugar and salt together. Add egg yolks to mixture.

Boil 1 ½ c. water in microwave and add slowly to a mixture of cocoa and flour, keeping lump free. Put in microwave in bowl, cover with waxed paper and cook 1 – 2 minutes at a time, stirring thoroughly between times until mixture thickens. Add 1 tsp. vanilla and let cool before putting in a baked pie crust.

For best meringue, beat 3 egg whites with mixer. Add 4 tbsp. sugar slowly. Take other 2 tbsp. sugar, 1 tbsp. cornstarch and ½ c. cold water and cook in pan, stirring constantly until thickened. Cool. Add to the egg white mixture and beat until blended well. Cook at 350 degrees until golden brown (12-15 minutes). This makes meringue hold up for several days in refrigerator, and cuts well.

Ann Floyd

"TIP OF THE HAT"

Notes...

Strolling down memory lane, we extend a **"TIP OF THE HAT"** *to what was once a long-time landmark in Franklin...*

Herbert's Bar-B-Q Restaurant

We do this in memory of **Mr. Wilson Herbert,** friend and family to many of us over the years, by sharing with you a few of his menu's featured recipes.

HERBERT'S BAR-B-Q SAUCE

1 lb. butter
8 oz. Worcestershire sauce
6 oz. minced onion
4 oz. garlic powder
6 oz. black pepper
1 gal. tomato catsup
2 oz. celery salt
1 gallon white vinegar
8 oz. lemon juice
4 oz. garlic salt
16 oz. brown sugar
4 oz. mild red pepper*
8 oz. salt
2 tsp. dry mustard

* "If you want it hot, just add more hot red pepper"

Mix all ingredients in large dutch oven. Bring to boil over medium heat while stirring. Simmer at least 5 minutes. Makes approximately 2 ½ gallons.

(This recipe was given to Herbert's by J. D. "Punkin" Porter, from Thompson Station, when the restaurant was opened in 1986.)

HERBERT'S CHESS PIE

1 tbsp. apple cider vinegar
1 tsp. vanilla extract
1 c. sugar
4 eggs, slightly beaten
8 unbaked tart shells
1 tbsp. light corn syrup
½ c. melted butter or margarine
1 tbsp. bourbon (optional)

Combine the vinegar, corn syrup, vanilla and melted butter in a medium bowl and mix well. Combine the sugar and butter mixture in a large bowl, stirring until well blended. Add the eggs and mix well. Stir in the bourbon. Pour into the tart shells.

Bake at 350 degrees for 25 to 30 minutes or until a knife inserted near the center comes out clean. Cool on a wire rack. May be prepared in a 9-inch pie shell and baked for 35 to 40 minutes. Yields 8.

HOT SLAW

Chop and mix together:

1 head cabbage or 1 pkg. already chopped cabbage
2 bell peppers
2 onions
1 head lettuce
4 tomatoes
4 or 5 sweet pickles
3 stalks celery

Combine the following and pour over the above mixture:

1 c. vinegar
1 large bottle catsup (32 oz.)
1 c. sugar
cayenne pepper (hot)

(Use the cayenne pepper according to just how hot you want the slaw to be. This can be made a day or night ahead and stored in the refrigerator. It keeps for weeks.)

JUST A FEW MORE

Notes...

CHAMPAGNE FRUIT

Mix together and chill:

5 c. seasonal fruit (strawberries, cantaloupe, pineapple, apples, peaches, mandarin oranges, berries)
¼ c. honey

Before serving, add 2 tbsp. Triple Sec and 6 ½ oz. champagne. Garnish with mint.

Christi Smith
(Our daughter)

CHEESE SOUFFLE

8 slices white bread. Trim crusts and pull slices in pieces.
3 c. milk
Sprinkle of cayenne pepper
8 oz. cheddar cheese, grated
4 beaten eggs
1 tsp. Worcestershire sauce

Mix ingredients well and pour into an 8x8 inch casserole dish that has been sprayed with Pam. Cover and place in refrigerator overnight. When ready to bake place in a moderate oven and cook until it is puffy and light brown. The guests have to wait on this dish, for it will not wait on them.. It has to be served immediately when it comes out of the oven. People always enjoy this delicious fondue or soufflé.

I have learned to put it in a very slow oven if I can't be sure when we will eat. That way, after it is hot all the way through, it can be hurried somewhat after everyone has arrived.

Virginia Bowman

CURRIED FRUIT

1 can pears (16 oz.)
1 can pineapple chunks (16 oz.)
3 sliced bananas
¾ c. brown sugar
1 tsp. ginger
1 can peach halves (16 oz.)
½ c. sliced cherries
1/3 c. butter
2 tsp. curry powder

Drain fruit and place in large casserole dish. Melt butter and add sugar and spices, then mix well. Pour butter mixture over fruit. Bake covered in 325 degree oven for 1 hour. Serve HOT. Serves 10-12.

Cheryl Wilson

FRUIT BAKE

1 lb. can peaches, pears, pineapple chunks, purple plums, apricots, and applesauce.

1 c. maraschino cherries
½ c. sugar
1/3 c. butter

Drain fruit. Mix applesauce, butter, and sugar. Add a pinch of cinnamon, and ginger. Bring to boil.

Layer fruit in casserole. Top with apple sauce mixture. Let stand overnight. Bake 45 minutes at 350 degrees. Remove from oven and sprinkle immediately over top 3 tbsp. brown sugar and ½ cup pecans.

Serve at room temperature.

Nadine Smithson

JELLO CRANBERRY RELISH

2 ½ c. orange juice
1 c. assorted dried fruit
(I use apricots, raisins,
chopped dates)
1 tbsp. grated lemon peel
(optional)
1 small pkg. cranberry jello
1 tsp. ground cinnamon
¼ tsp. ground cloves
1 c. toasted walnuts
(I sometimes use plain ones.)

Dissolve orange juice and jello on stove. Add remaining ingredients and put in refrigerator. Even good on buttered biscuits.

Ann Inman

LEMON MAYONNAISE

Beat together:

1 egg
¾ c. sugar
½ c. fruit juice (pineapple)
juice of ½ lemon
1 tbsp. flour

Stir until boils. Cool.

Great dressing for Christmas fruit salad.

"MAMIE"

PEAR HONEY

1 can crushed pineapple with syrup (20 oz.)
8 c. (about 3 lbs.) peeled, cored, and chopped pears
10 c. sugar
1 tbsp. lemon juice

Mix all ingredients and cook until pears are tender and mixture thickens, approximately 30 minutes. Place in sterilized jars and seal while still hot.

Carolyn Pratt

TOMATO PIE

1 deep dish piecrust
2 tomatoes, sliced
1- 1 ½ c. grated cheddar cheese
2 eggs, lightly beaten
salt & pepper
1 small onion, chopped
½ pt. whipping cream
3 slices provolone cheese
fresh basil, to taste
olive oil

Place the raw chopped onions in the bottom of the piecrust. Salt, pepper and flour the tomatoes and brown in a little olive oil. Place on top of the onions. Place the cheddar cheese and provolone cheese over the tomatoes and onions, then pour the eggs over that mixture. Pour the whipping cream over the whole pie and place a small amount of fresh basil on top. Bake at 350 degrees for approximately 1 hour. It is best to put something under the pie because it might boil over. Watch – and once it is firm, it is done.

(This recipe came from my mother and it is delicious in the summer with fresh Bradley tomatoes.

Melissa Davis

UNCOOKED RELISH

1 pt. sweet red peppers
1 pt. sweet green peppers
2 tsp. celery seed
1 qt. vinegar (I use a little more)
5 tbsp. salt
1 qt. cabbage, chopped
1 pt. white onions, chopped
4 c. sugar (I use 4 ½)
2 or 3 hot peppers

Put each vegetable through a food chopper. I use fine blade – calls for coarse blade. Drain each real well and discard liquid. Measure each after chopping.

Mix vegetables with salt and let stand overnight. Next morning, drain off as much liquid as possible. (Press down with palm of hand). Add spices, sugar and vinegar to vegetables and mix well. Pack in sterilized Kerr jars to within ½ inch of top. Put on cap. Screw band firmly tight. Process in boiling water bath for 15 minutes. Yields 5-6 pints.

Catherine Pratt

VEGETARIAN SWEET AND SOUR MEATBALLS

My son and his family are vegetarians and this is very good – even if you aren't a vegetarian.

4 eggs
½ c. finely chopped onion
1 c. finely chopped pecans
1 ½ tsp. salt
2 c. Italian bread crumbs
1 c. shredded cheddar cheese
½ c. cottage cheese
1 tsp. dried basil
¼ tsp. dried sage

SWEET & SOUR SAUCE:
¼ c. vegetable oil
¾ c. apricot jam
¼ c. minced onion
dash hot pepper sauce
¼ c. white vinegar
1 c. ketchup
1 tsp. oregano

(Continued on next page)

Preheat oven to 350 degrees. In a large bowl, mix together the eggs, cheese and cottage cheese until well blended. Mix in ½ c. onion, pecans, basil, salt and sage. Stir in bread crumbs.

Form the mixture in 2 inch balls and place them in a 9x13 inch baking dish. In another bowl, whisk together the vegetable oil, vinegar, apricot jam, ketchup, ¼ c. onion, oregano and hot sauce. Pour over meatballs. Bake uncovered for 35 – 40 minutes until meatballs are firm and the sauce is thick and bubbly.

Incredibly delicious, serve as a main course or an appetizer.

Marjorie Hernandez

VEGGIE PIZZA

2 cans crescent rolls
1 c. mayonnaise
2 (8 oz.) cream cheese (softened)
1 c. raw broccoli, chopped
1 tomato, chopped
1 c. shredded cheddar cheese
1 pkg. Hidden Valley Ranch mix
1 c. raw carrots, chopped
1 green pepper, chopped

Spread can crescent rolls on cookie sheet, bake and cool. Mix Hidden Valley Ranch mix, mayonnaise and cream cheese together and spread over cooked crescent rolls. Sprinkle remaining ingredients and refrigerate overnight.

Angie Bascle

"CHRISTMAS TREES"

To preserve evergreen Christmas trees, mix together:

2 c. sugar
2 tbsp. Clorox
1 gallon water

Pour in container and allow tree to stand in mixture 2 days. This treatment will prevent tree from becoming so brittle and shedding.

"HO! HO! HO!"

Brent Sanders

INDEX

Salads & Dressings (con.)

Soups, Stews and Chili, Too

Sweet Stuff – Cakes

Sweet Stuff – Candy, Brownies, Etc.

Just A Few More

Real Estate

7065 Moores Lane
Brentwood, TN 37027
615-370-4663
www.mcarthursanders.com